FIRES

by Marguerite Yourcenar

FIRES

*Marguerite Yourcenar
Translated from the
French by Dori Katz
in collaboration with
the author*

The University of Chicago Press

Published by arrangement with Farrar, Straus and Giroux, Inc.

The University of Chicago Press, Chicago 60637

Printed in the United States of America

01 00 99 98 97 96 95 94   6 5 4 3 2 1

ISBN 0-226-96528-7 (pbk.)

Library of Congress Cataloging-in-Publication Data

Yourcenar, Marguerite.
    [Feux. English]
    Fires / Marguerite Yourcenar ; translated from the French by Dori
Katz in collaboration with the author.
       p.   cm.
    1. Mythology, Greek—Poetry. 2. Love—Poetry. 3. Monologues.
I. Katz, Dori. II. Title.
PQ2649.08F4   1994
841'.912—dc20   94–19775
                                           CIP

♾ The paper used in this publication meets the minimum requirements of
the American National Standard for Information Sciences— Permanence of
Paper for Printed Library Materials, ANSI Z39.48-1984.

To Hermes

———————

CONTENTS

PREFACE

Fires is not, properly speaking, a book of my youth: it was written in 1935; I was thirty-two. The work, published in 1936, was reissued in 1957 with almost no change; neither has anything been changed in the text of this edition.

The product of a love crisis, *Fires* is in the form of a collection of love poems, or, rather, is like a sequence of lyrical prose pieces connected by a notion of love. As such, the book does not require any commentary. Absolute love, striking its victim both as a disease and as a vocation, has been, from time immemorial, a common experience and one of the most hackneyed themes of literature. At the most, what is to be noted is that all love experienced, like that which inspired this book, is done and undone within a given situation through a complicated combination of feelings and circumstances. In a novel these would be woven into the plot, and in a poem these are the starting point of song. In *Fires*, these feelings and circumstances are expressed sometimes directly, if rather cryptically, in unrelated *pensées* that were at first notes for a private diary; sometimes, on the contrary, they are expressed indirectly through narratives borrowed from legends and history, and meant to serve the poet as props through time.

The mythical or real people in these stories, all except for Mary Magdalene, belong to ancient Greece; this was the Greece of the Syrian–Judaic world that formed Christianity, and which Renaissance and Baroque painters (perhaps in a more realistic vein than one would think) always loved to fill with beautiful classical architecture, with beautiful draperies and beautiful nudes. In various degrees, all these stories modernize the past. Furthermore, some are partly colored by the intermediary stages myths and legends have crossed to reach us; therefore, the so-called classical in *Fires* is often only a first hardly discernible layer. Phaedra is in no way the Athenian Phaedra; she is the passionate criminal we owe to Racine. Achilles and Patroclus are derived less from Homer than from the poets, the painters, and the sculptors ranging from Homeric times to the present; these two stories, variegated here and there with twentieth-century colors, lead moreover to a timeless dream-like world. Antigone is taken straight from Greek drama, but of all the stories told in *Fires*, this nightmare of civil war and rebellion against iniquitous authority is perhaps the one most loaded with contemporary or quasi-anticipatory elements. Lena's story is based on the little we know about the courtesan of that name who participated in 525 B.C. in Harmodius and Aristogiton's plot, but local color of modern Greece and the obsessive civil wars of our times almost completely cover the sixth-century foundation. Clytemnestra's monologue blends Homeric Mycenae with a rustic landscape from the period of the Greek–Turkish conflict of 1924 or the fiasco of the Dardanelles. Phaedo's monologue comes out of remarks by Diogenes Laërtius on the adolescence of this student of Socrates; the night life of Athens in 1935 is projected against that enjoyed by privileged young men in Alcibiades' time. The Mary Magdalene story stems from a tradition mentioned in *The Golden Legend* (and furthermore rejected as unauthentic by the author of this pious collection)

that turned the saint into Saint John's betrothed;
she was abandoned by him and followed Christ.
Arising from the apocryphal Gospels, the Near
East evoked in the story is from yesterday and
from always, but metaphors and *double-entendres*
introduce, here and there, modern anachronisms.
Sappho's adventure is connected to Greece through
the contested legend of the poetess's suicide over a
handsome, unresponsive youth, but this Sappho–
acrobat belongs to the international world of
pleasure-seekers between the wars, and the impersonation incident is related more to Shakespearean
comedies than to Greek themes. Everywhere in
Fires a very deliberate bias of superimpression
mingles the past to a present that has, in turn,
become the past.

Every book bears the stamp of its age, as it
should. This is accomplished in two ways: first,
by the coloring and the odor of the times that
permeate more or less the author's life; second, by
the complicated play of literary influences and
the reactions against them, especially when the
author is still young; it is not always easy to distinguish between one or the other form of influence. I will readily admit, in "Phaedo, or the

Dance," the influence of that voluptuous human-ism of Paul Valéry, although here its beautiful surface is veiled by a vehemence very unlike Valéry.* The violence of *Fires* reacts, consciously or not, against Giraudoux, whose ingenious and Parisian Greece irritated me as something can when it is both very close and totally opposed to us. Today I see that the common modern taste for transposing antiquity hardly distinguishes, except for the most attentive reader, between Giraudoux's world, which is solidly anchored in French tradi-tion, and the more frenzied world I was trying to paint. On the other hand, I liked Cocteau; I ap-preciated his gifts as a mystifier and sorcerer, but I did not like the way he often lowered himself with conjurer's tricks and sleights of hand. The arrogant frankness of the person speaking in *Fires*, with or without mask, the insolent will to address only the acquired or conquered reader, represent a defense against certain skillful and casual com-promises. Cocteau's precedent encouraged me to

* A reference to the "admirable Paul" in the first group of *pensées* attests to that interest in Valéry's work. This *pensée* turns upside down a remark of Paul Valéry in *Choses Tues*, 1932.

use the very old device of the lyrical pun that was also being rediscovered in those days, and, in a different way, by the surrealists. I don't think I would have dared these verbal overloads, which in *Fires* correspond to the thematic superimpression I mentioned earlier, if poets of my time, and not just of the past, hadn't given me the example. Other similarities to contemporaries come from, as I said before, life itself.

The love of spectacles shared by the generation that in 1935 was about thirty years old took the triple aspects of ballet, music hall, and film. Thus, in "Achilles, or the Lie," the typically dreamlike descent of Misandra and Achilles down the staircase of the tower evokes a flying rehearsal of the half-winged acrobat Barbette dragging behind him the classical veils of Greek Victories. (I was destined to run into him in Florida, where, half deformed by a terrible fall, he was teaching his art to the equilibrists of the Barnum circus.) It also explains why, in "Phaedo, or the Dance," a cabaret dance is allied to the dance of the stars. In "Patroclus, or Destiny," the duel between Achilles and the Amazon is a baroque ballet seen through Diaghilev or Massine, and is shot by the cameras of filmmakers; it is also characteristic of this period of games mixed with war anguish. In "Antigone, or the Choice," by a foreshadowing that is also typical of the times, the spotlights following in the book the movements of a character are already on their way to becoming the lugubrious searchlights of concentration camps. This sensitivity to the political danger weighing on the world left undeniable marks on certain poets and novelists of the thirties; it is normal that *Fires*, like any other book of those days, should contain the shadows of these forthcoming events.

A deeper analysis of the book would probably only yield purely biographical residues: it may be important only to me that "Sappho, or the Suicide" came from seeing a variety show in Pera, and that the phrase was written on the deck of a cargo ship moored on the Bosphorus, while the gramophone of a friend played for hours on end a popular American refrain, "He flies through the air with the greatest of ease/This daring young man on the flying trapeze." Perhaps it also doesn't matter much that these ingredients are, in the legend of the classical poetess, mingled with memories of impersonations during the Renaissance, and are mingled also with echoes of lines of poetry, the only good ones I know by that whimsical virtuoso Banville, when he speaks of a clown thrown in mid-sky; mingled also with a recollection of an admirable Degas drawing. Finally, these ingredients were also mixed with a certain number of cosmopolitan silhouettes in Constantinople bars in those days. For the benefit of the strictly literary exegesis, I might mention that the Athens in *Fires* is the city where my early-morning walks in the old Ceramicus cemetery, with its weeds and neglected tombstones, were orchestrated by the squeaky noise of a neighboring streetcar yard; the city where fortune-tellers living in shantytowns predicted the future by reading Turkish coffee grounds; the city where a small group of young men and women, some of whom were soon destined to a quick or slow death, would end the long idle night with discussions on the Spanish Civil War or the respective merits of competing German or Swedish movie stars. Afterwards, slightly drunk on wine and the Oriental music of taverns, they would go to look at the sun rising on the Parthenon. Through a possibly banal optical effect, these people, who represented then contemporary reality, seem to me today more removed and abolished by time than the myths and obscure legends that personify them.

Stylistically, *Fires* belongs to the ornate and tight mannerism that I adopted in that period and that alternated with the almost excessively discreet one of the classical story. Equally distant today from one as from the other, I discussed elsewhere what are still for me the virtues of the classical French narrative: its abstract expression of passion, the apparent or real control it imposes on the author. Without discussing the merits or demerits of *Fires*, I would like to say that the almost excessive expressionism of these poems still seems to me to be a form of natural and needed confession, a legitimate effort to portray the full complexity and passion of an emotion. This tendency, persisting or reemerging at all times in literature, in spite of wise puristic or classical restrictions, stubbornly, maybe nightmarishly, tries to create an entirely poetic language, one in which each word, loaded with maximum meaning, would reveal its hidden significances in the way phosphorescences of stones are revealed under certain lights. The poet always wants to put feelings or ideas in concrete forms, in forms that may have become in themselves *pre-*

cious (the very term is revealing), like those gems that owe their density and sparkle to the almost unbearable pressures and temperatures they've been through. Better still, he wishes to wring out of language the skillful twisting of Renaissance ironworks whose complex interlacings were at first molten iron. The worst that can be said for those daring verbal plays is that the writer who uses them continually risks abuse and excess, as any writer devoted to classical understatement always brushes against the danger of cold elegance or hypocrisy.

If the reader often sees only preciousness, in the bad sense of the word, in what I would willingly call baroque expressionism, it's that nine times out of ten the poet yielded to a wish to startle, to please or displease above everything else. Sometimes, though, it is because this same reader cannot follow, all the way through, the idea or emotion that the poet is giving, so that he mistakenly takes it as a forced metaphor or a strained conceit. It is not Shakespeare's fault but ours that, when the poet compares his lover to a grave "hung with the trophies of my lovers gone" (Sonnet XXXI), we do not see in this tomb decked out with the pennants of his passion the banners of Elizabethan times fluttering around us. It's not Racine's fault but ours if the famous line "Consumed by more fires than I ignited," pronounced by a Pyrrhus in love with Andromache, does not show us the immense conflagration of burning Troy behind this despairing lover, and if, in what appears to cultured readers a flat simile unworthy of the great Racine, we do not feel the dark introspective musings of a man who has been pitiless and who begins to learn what suffering is like. In this line of poetry, Racine, by a method he often uses, revives the metaphor of the fires of love, already a cliché in his day, and gives it back the luster of real flames; this line also brings us back to the technique of the lyrical pun that draws in a single word the two branches of a parable. If, to get back to *Fires*, Phaedra to go down to Hell takes the "oars" (rails) that are both those of Charon the ferryman and those of the Metro, it's because during rush hours this human swell pouring into the underground corridors of our cities is perhaps for us the most terrifying image of the river of the dead. (The lyrical pun is lost in English, since there is not a single word that means both "oar" and "rail," but the metaphor can still be evoked by words here that suggest sailing on dark waters.) In the same way, if Thetis is both the mother of Achilles and the divinity of the waves, this lyrical punning on the words *mer/mère* blends into one image the double aspects of the goddess. This pun is only possible in French, since the word for sea, *mer*, sounds the same as the word for mother, *mère*. I could cite many more such examples in *Fires*, but the important thing is to try to show that these games (where the meaning of a word plays on its syntactical context) are not a form of deliberate affectation or wit, but, as in the Freudian slip or the double or triple association of ideas in madness or dream, these are poetic reflexes to a theme particularly rich in emotion and dangers for the author. In one of my more recent works, one that is the furthest removed from stylistic experimentation and play, I spontaneously named—without realizing that I was punning—the warden of the prison where my hero was dying, Herman Mohr; that is, Mr. Man (Herr Mann), in German, of death (*mort*) in French.

No matter how often I say that a collection of love poems does not require commentary (which is true in principle), I know that I seem to be avoiding the issue in dealing at such great length with thematic and stylistic characteristics while keeping quiet about the love experience that inspired the book. But, besides feeling the ridiculous position that I'm in, commenting on a book that I did not wish read, this is not the place to discuss whether this total love for a particular person, with all the risk it holds for the lover and the loved, with its inevitable deception, its authentic abnegation and humility, and also its latent violence and selfish demands, whether this love is worthy or not of the exalted place the poets gave it. What seems obvious is that this notion of mad, sometimes scandalous love that is nevertheless permeated by a sort of mystical power could only survive if it is associated with whatever belief in transcendence, even if only within a human being. If deprived of this basis of metaphysical and moral values (which are spurned today perhaps because our predecessors abused them), mad love quickly becomes nothing more than vain mirror play or sad mania. In *Fires*, where I thought I was only glorifying or perhaps exorcising a very concrete love, the worshipping of the person loved is very clearly associated with more abstract but no less intense notions, and these no-

tions sometimes prevail over the carnal and senti-
mental obsession: in "Antigone, or the Choice,"
Antigone's choice is that of justice; in "Phaedo, or
the Dance," the dance is knowledge; in "Mary
Magdalene, or Salvation," salvation is God. It is
not a question of sublimation, which is in itself a
very unfortunate term and one that insults the
body, but a dark perception that love for a particular person, so poignant, is often only a beautiful fleeting accident, less real in a way than the pre-
dispositions and choices that preceded it and that
will outlive it. Through the dash and unconstraint
of these sort of quasi-public confessions, certain
passages in *Fires* seem to me to contain today truths
glimpsed early on that needed a whole lifetime to
be rediscovered and authenticated. For me, this
masked ball was only a stage of awareness.

M.Y., 1975

FIRES

I hope this book will never be read.

There is between us something better than love: a complicity.

Absent, your face expands so that it fills the universe. You reach the fluid state which is the one of ghosts. Present, your face condenses, you achieve the concentration of the heaviest metals, of iridium, of mercury. This weight kills me when it falls on my heart.

The admirable Paul was wrong (I am speaking of the great sophist, Paul Valéry, and not of the predicator). There is for each thought, for each love that if left alone would perhaps fail, a singularly strong stimulant—the ENTIRE REST OF THE WORLD—*which is opposed to it and is not worthy of it.*

3

Loneliness . . . I don't believe as they do, I don't live as they do, I don't love as they do . . . I will die as they die.

Alcohol sobers me. After a few swallows of brandy, I no longer think of you.

PHAEDRA

OR DESPAIR

P haedra settles everything. She abandons her mother to the bull, her sister to loneliness: she is uninterested in these kinds of love. She leaves her country like someone giving up dreams: she disowns her family like someone pawning memories. Living where innocence is a crime, she witnesses with disgust what she will end up being. Seen from the outside, her destiny horrifies her: right now she knows it only through the inscriptions on the Labyrinth's wall: she escapes from her terrible future by running away. She marries Theseus as absentmindedly as Saint Mary of Egypt paid the price of passage with her body. She lets the gigantic slaughterhouses of her American Crete sink in the West behind her, in a fog of fables. She lands, permeated with the odor of the ranch and of fish from Haiti, unsuspectingly carrying the leprosy contracted in a torrid-heart Tropic. Her astonishment upon seeing Hippolytus is that of a traveler who unknowingly has retraced her steps: the boy's profile recalls Knossos and the Cretan two-edged ax. She hates him, she raises him; he grows up against her, rebuffed by her hatred, accustomed, since his early years, to mistrust women, forced since school to skip over obstacles an inimical stepmother has raised. She is jealous of his arrows—his victims, of his companions—his solitude. In this virgin forest which is Hippolytus' domain, she unwillingly plants the signposts of Minos' palace; she traces through the underbrush the one-way road leading to Fatality. She creates and re-creates Hippolytus; her love is a true incest; she cannot kill this youth without a sort of infanticide. She manufactures his beauty, his chastity, his weaknesses, extracting these from deep within herself; to be able to hate it under the guise of an insipid virgin, she removes his detestable purity; his nonexistent Aricia is wrought from scratch. She gets drunk on the impossible, the heady basis of all mixtures of misfortunes. In Theseus' bed she has the bitter pleasure of cheating, in actuality, on the man she loves, and, in imagination, on the one she doesn't. She becomes a mother: she has children as she would have remorse. Feverish between her damp sheets, she comforts herself by whispering confessions like a child mumbling secrets on her nurse's neck; she suckles her unhappiness; at last she becomes Phaedra's downtrodden servant. Confronting Hippolytus' coldness, she imitates the sun coming up against crystal: she turns into a specter; she haunts her body as if it were her personal hell. She re-creates inside herself a deep Labyrinth where she is bound to dwell again; Ariadne's thread will not pull her out, since she winds it around her heart. She is widowed; at last she can weep without being asked why. But black does not become this dark figure; she begrudges her mourning because it falsifies her grief. Rid of Theseus, she carries her hope like a shameful posthumous pregnancy. To forget herself, she becomes involved in intrigues; she accepts the Regency as she would begin to knit a shawl. Theseus returns too late to bring her back into the world of routine he lives in; she can enter it only through the opening of a subterfuge: rapture by rapture, she imagines the rape Hippolytus will be accused of, so that her lie becomes her fulfillment. She is telling the truth: she has been raped; her imposture is a translation. She takes poison, since gradually she has become immune to her own; Hippolytus' disappearance creates a void around her; drawn into this void, she is engulfed by death. She confesses before dying, to have the pleasure, for the last time, of talking about her crime. Without changing places, she returns to the family palace where sin is innocence. Pushed by the throng of her ancestors, she slides along these subway corridors filled with animal smells; here oars split the oily waters of the Styx, here shiny rails suggest either suicide or departure. At the bottom of the mining galleries of her underground Crete, she will undoubtedly end up meeting the young man disfigured by her claws, since she has all the detours of eternity to find him. She has not seen him since the fatal scene of Act Three; it's because of him that she is dead; it's because of her that he did not live; he owes her only death; she owes him the convulsions of an irrepressible agony. She has the right to hold him responsible for her crime, for blackening her immortality now that poets will use her name for their own incestuous desires, in the same way that a driver lying on the road with a broken skull can hold the tree he has smashed against responsible;

like all victims, he was his own torturer. At last, definitive words will come from her lips no longer trembling with hope. What will she say? Perhaps, thank you.

On a plane, next to you, I am no longer afraid. One
dies only alone.

I will never be beaten. I would only be beaten by
winning. Since every foiled plot encloses me in a
love that will, in the long run, be my grave, I will
end my life caught in my victories. Only defeat
finds keys, opens doors. Death, to reach the fugi-
tive, must be set in motion, lose this fixity that
makes us recognize in her the hard opposite of life.
Death gives us the end of the swan struck in full
flight, of Achilles grabbed by the hair by who
knows what dark Wisdom. As for the woman asphyxiated in the entrance hall of her house in
Pompeii, Death only prolongs the corridors of escape into the other world. My own death will be
of stone. I am familiar with gangways, drawbridges,
traps, with all the underground passages of Fatality.

I cannot get lost. Death, to kill me, will need me as an accomplice.

Have you noticed how men, when shot down, collapse, fall on their knees? Bodies slack in spite of the ropes, they cave in as if fainting in afterthought. They do as I do. They adore their death.

There is no unhappy love: you only possess what you don't possess. There is no happy love: what you possess, you possess no longer.

Nothing to fear. I've touched bottom. I cannot sink lower than your heart.

ACHILLES

O R T H E L I E

All lamps had been extinguished. In the low-ceilinged dark room, servants were weaving a surprising web that was to become the Fates'; a useless embroidery hung from Achilles' hands. You could no longer tell Misandra's black gown from Deidamia's red one; Achilles' white gown was green in the moonlight. Since the arrival of this young stranger in whom all women sensed a god, fear had slipped into the Island like a shadow lying under Beauty's feet. Daylight was no longer day but a blond mask placed on darkness; women's breasts became chest plates on young soldiers. As soon as Thetis saw the film of battles Achilles would die in, a vision being formed in Jupiter's eyes, she sought in all the seas of the world an island, a rock, a bed so water-tight that it could float toward the future. This stormy goddess had broken the underground cables that transmitted the battle's commotion to the Island, blinded the eye of the beacon guiding ships, chased away the migratory birds that brought her son messages from brothers-in-arms. Like peasant women putting their sick boys in women's dresses to dodge Fever, she had dressed him in her goddess tunics to mislead Death. This son infected with mortality reminded her of the only sin of her divine younger years; she had slept with a man without taking the banal precaution of changing him into a god. You could see in the boy the father's coarse traits invested with a beauty that could only come from her and that would make dying someday even more painful. Sheathed in silk, veiled in gauze, entangled in gold necklaces, Achilles, following her orders, had sneaked into the maiden's tower; he had just come out of the Centaurs' College: weary of woods, he dreamed of flowing hair; tired of hard chests, he dreamed of breasts. The feminine shelter his mother had locked him into became for this dodger a sublime adventure; protected by a corset or a dress, he could penetrate the vast unexplored continent of women, where, up to now, man had only come as conqueror under the gleaming of love conflagrations. Like a turncoat coming from the male camp, Achilles could take the unique chance here to be someone other than himself. To the slaves, he belonged to the asexual race of masters; Deidamia's father's aberration loved in him the virgin he wasn't; only his two cousins refused to believe in this girl too like the ideal image men have of women. Unfamiliar with the realities of love, the boy began in Deidamia's bed the apprenticeship of struggles, of gasping, of subterfuges; his swooning on this tender victim was a substitute for a more terrible, unseizable, anonymous rapture which was Death. Deidamia's love, Misandra's jealousy re-created in him the hard opposite of a girl. Passions undulated in the tower like scarves tormented by the breeze; Achilles and Deidamia hated each other like lovers; Misandra and Achilles loved each other like enemies. This athletic adversary became for Achilles the equivalent of a brother; this delightful rival moved Misandra like a sort of sister. Each wave landing on the Island brought messages: Greek corpses pushed into the open sea by unheard-of winds were the debris of an army wrecked for want of Achilles' assistance. Searchlights disguised as stars looked for him in the sky. Fame and war perceived in the misty future seemed to him like demanding mistresses whose possession would involve too many crimes: he thought that in this women's prison he could escape the solicitations of his victims-to-be. A bark loaded with kings stopped at the foot of the dead beacon that had become one more dangerous reef: Ulysses, Patroclus, Thersites, warned by an anonymous letter, had announced their visit to the princesses; Misandra, suddenly complaisant, helped Deidamia pin up Achilles' hair. Her big hands were trembling as though she had just let a secret slip through her fingers. The huge open door brought in the night, the kings, the wind, the sky full of signs. Worn out by the thousand steps he had climbed, Thersites was panting and rubbing his rheumatic knees between his hands. He looked like a king who through stinginess would be his own buffoon. Patroclus, hesitating as though in a game of hide-and-seek, stretched out his iron-gloved hands haphazardly toward the young women. Ulysses' head made one think of a used, pared, rusted coin on which you could still detect the features of the king of Ithaca; hands shielding his eyes as though he were at the top of a mast, he was examining the princesses leaning

against the wall like a group of statues: Misandra's
short hair, her big hands shaking the leaders', her
ease, made him at first mistake her for the hiding
place of a male. The sailors of the escort unpacked
the boxes and took out the jewelry, the enamel
toilet kits, and the weapons Achilles would undoubtedly hurry to brandish. But the helmets handled by the six manicured hands recalled hoods of
hair dryers; pliant sword belts were transformed
into sashes; in Deidamia's arms a shield looked like
a cradle. Disguises, like an inescapable bad spell
on the Island, were everywhere; gold became silver-
gilt, sailors transvestites, and the two kings door-
to-door salesmen. Only Patroclus was immune to
the charm, breaking it like a bared sword. A cry
of admiration from Deidamia called him to Achilles'
attention; the latter leaped toward him, took the
hard head chiseled like the pommel of a sword
between his hands, not realizing that his veils, his
bracelets, his rings transformed his gesture into
the transport of an amorous woman. Loyalty,
friendship, heroism ceased being words used by
hypocrites to hide their inner souls; loyalty was
these eyes remaining clear before the heap of lies;
friendship would be their hearts; fame their double

future. Blushing, Patroclus rebuffed this feminine embrace: Achilles stepped back, let his arms hang, shed tears that only perfected his girlish disguise but gave Deidamia a new reason to prefer Patroclus. Achilles' confusion turned into mad jealousy when he noted the side glances, the meaningful smiles, the embarrassment of the young ensign half submerged by this flood of laces. The young man girded in bronze eclipsed the night images Deidamia had of Achilles; in her woman's eyes, a uniform surpassed the pale brightness of a nude body. Achilles clumsily seized a sword and immediately dropped it; then, like a girl spiteful of the success of her friend, he used his hands to squeeze Deidamia's neck. The eyes of the strangled woman burst out, looking like two big tears; slaves intervened; doors closing with a musical sound muffled Deidamia's last gasps: disconcerted, the kings found themselves on the other side of the threshold. The women's quarters were filled with a suffocating obscurity unrelated to night. Kneeling, Achilles listened to Deidamia's life spilling slowly out of her throat like water from a vase's too narrow neck. He felt more separated than ever from this woman he had tried not only to possess but to be: as he loosened his grip, the enigma of death was added to the mystery of womanhood. He ran his hands alongside her body and felt her breasts, her sides, her unadorned hair with horror. He rose, groped along the smooth walls, ashamed not to have recognized in the kings the secret emissaries of his own courage, certain to have let slip his only chance to be a god. The stars, Misandra's revenge, Deidamia's father's indignation, all would unite now to keep him locked up in this palace with no frontage on fame: now his comings and goings around this corpse would be like standing still. He felt hands almost as cold as Deidamia's land on his shoulder: startled, he heard Misandra suggest that he flee before the wrath of her omnipotent father burst on him. He entrusted his wrist to this fatal friend's hand, fell into step behind this girl knowing her way in the shadows; he wondered whether Misandra was yielding to a rancor or a dark gratitude, whether his guide was a woman taking revenge or a woman he had revenged. Doors unfolded, then folded on them: worn floor tiles gave softly under their feet like the limp hollow of a wave; Achilles and Misandra pursued their spiral-like descent faster and faster as though their dizziness were a weight dragging them down. Misandra was keeping track of the number of steps like someone counting out loud the beads of a stone chaplet. At last a door opened on the cliffs, the seawall, the lighthouse stairs; air, salty as blood and tears, rushed to the faces of this strange couple startled by the invigorating coolness. With a hard laugh, Misandra stopped the handsome creature gathering his skirts, already set to leap, and gave him a mirror in which daybreak would let him see his face; had she consented to lead him into daylight only to inflict upon him the pale and painted reflection of his godlike emptiness? But this marble pallor, this hair waving like the mane on a helmet, this makeup mixed with tears that stuck to his cheeks like blood from a wound—all this, on the contrary, gathered in the narrow frame every forthcoming aspect of Achilles, as though this small piece of glass had captured the future. The sunlike creature tore off his belt, untied his scarf; he was going to remove his cumbersome muslins but was stopped by the fear of being more exposed to the guards' fire if he rashly showed himself nude. For a moment, the hardest of these two divine women leaned

over the world, contemplating taking on her own
shoulders the weight of Achilles' destiny, of burning Troy, of Patroclus avenged, since the most
discerning of gods or butchers could not have dis-
tinguished this man's heart from her own. Prisoner
of her breasts, Misandra opened the double doors
that seemed to groan for her own destiny, and with
her elbow she shoved Achilles out toward everything she would never be. The doors closed on this
woman buried alive. Released like an eagle,
Achilles ran along the ramps, tumbled down the
steps, rushed down the ramparts, leapt over precipices, glided like an arrow, flew like a Victory. The
edges of rocks tore his clothes without scratching
his invulnerable flesh: the agile creature stopped,
untied his sandals, giving his naked soles the
chance to be wounded. The squadron was weighing anchor; siren calls crossed each other on the
sea. Raked by the wind, the sand hardly recorded
Achilles' light feet. Ready for departure, a boat
bristling with war machines was moored to the
breakwater, its chain stretched tight by the under-
tow. As though protected by a white cloud of sea
gulls coming from his marine Mother, Achilles
started walking on this fated cable, arms spread

out, held up by the wings of his floating scarfs. With one leap, this disheveled girl in whom a god was emerging landed in the back of the boat. Startled, the sailors knelt and greeted the arrival of Victory with a spray of profanity. Patroclus opened his arms, thinking he recognized Deidamia; Ulysses shook his head; Thersites burst out laughing. No one suspected this goddess of not being a woman.

A heart is perhaps something unsavory. It's on the order of anatomy tables and butcher's stalls. I prefer your body.

There is around us the atmosphere of Leysin, of Montana, of high mountain sanatoria glassed in like an aquarium, gigantic reserves where Death keeps coming to fish. The patients spit out bloodied confessions, trade bacilli, compare fever charts, settle into a friendship of danger signals. Between you and me, who has the most cavities?

Where shall I run to? You fill the world. I can only escape you in you.

Destiny is lighthearted. He who lends Fatality whatever beautiful mask knows it only through theatrical disguises. An unknown practical joker repeats the same vulgar seesaw, ad nauseam, until the death struggle. Chance is surrounded by a floating odor of children's rooms, of toy boxes which release the demons of Habit, of closets from which our maids, ludicrously dressed, sprang, hoping to make us scream. The Tragic characters jump up, brutally startled by booming, thunderous laughter. All his life, before losing his sight, Oedipus did nothing but play blindman's buff with Chance.

No matter how I change, my luck does not change. Any figure can be drawn within a circle.

We remember our dreams: we do not remember our sleep. Only twice did I enter these depths crossed by currents; there our dreams are only wreckage of submerged realities. The other day, drunk with happiness as you can be drunk with fresh air after a long race, I threw myself on my bed like a diver falling backwards, arms spread: I toppled over in a blue sea. Leaning against the abyss like a swimmer floating, and held up by the oxygen bag of my lungs full of air, I emerged from this Greek sea like a newborn island. Tonight, glutted with unhappiness, I drop into bed like a drowning woman letting go: I yield to sleep as though yielding to asphyxiation. Streams of memories persist through stupefied nocturnal weariness, dragging me toward an Asphaltic lake. There is no way to sink into this salt-saturated water, bitter as eyelid secretions. I am floating like the mummy in its bitumen, in fear of an awakening that at the very most will be a survival. The flux, then reflux of sleep bring me back, in spite of myself, to this batiste beach. My knees continually bump against your memory. The cold awakens me as though I had slept next to someone dead.

I bear your faults. One is resigned to God's faults. I bear your lacks. One is resigned to God's lacks.

A child is a hostage. Life has you. The same holds true of a dog, a panther, or a cicada. Leda would say: "I am no longer free· to kill myself since I bought a swan."

PATROCLUS

OR DESTINY

Night—or rather, a vague daylight—was falling on the flat, open country; you couldn't tell which way twilight was heading. Towers seemed like rocks, foothills seemed like towers. Painfully giving birth to the future, Cassandra was howling from atop the city walls. Blood stuck like rouge on the unrecognizable cheeks of corpses; Helen was painting her vampire mouth with lipstick that made one think of blood. Everyone had been settled there for years in a sort of red routine in which war and peace mingled like sand and water in stinking marsh regions. Harvested by armored trucks, the first generation of heroes had accepted war as a privilege, almost an investiture; they were followed, in turn, by a contingent of soldiers who accepted it as a duty and later bore it as a sacrifice. The invention of tanks made enormous gaps in these ranks now there

only as ramparts; a third wave of assailants stormed
death; staking their whole life, these gamblers fell
as though hit by their own ball right square in the
heart. Gone were the days of heroic tenderness,
when the adversary was the dark other side of the
friend. Iphigenia was dead, shot by Agamemnon's
order; she had been convicted of having had a
hand in the mutiny of the fleet. Paris had been
disfigured by the explosion of a grenade; Polyxena
had just succumbed to typhoid in Troy's hospital;
the Oceanids, kneeling on the beach, had given
up trying to keep the blue flies from Patroclus'
corpse. Since the death of this friend who had
first filled, then become his world, Achilles no
longer left his tent; it was littered with shadows:
naked, lying flat on the ground as though striving
to imitate the corpse, he let himself be eaten by
the vermin of his memories. More and more, death
seemed to him a sort of consecration only the purest
men were worthy of; many are undone, few die.
Thinking of Patroclus, he remembered the par-
ticularities: his paleness, the rigidity of his shoulders ever so slightly hunched, his hands always a
little cold, the weight of his body sinking into
sleep with the heaviness of a stone—all these

finally achieved their full meaning posthumously, as though, alive, Patroclus had only been the rough sketch of his corpse. The unavowed hatred sleeping in the bottom of love predisposed Achilles to the sculptor's task: he envied Hector for perfecting this masterpiece: only he, himself, should have torn away the last veils that thought, gesture, the very fact of being alive, placed between them, in order to discover Patroclus in the sublime nudity of his death. In vain did the Trojan chiefs have the horn blown, to announce skilled hand-to-hand combat now stripped of its early simplicity; widowed of this companion who deserved to be an enemy, Achilles did not kill any more, so as not to give Patroclus otherworldly rivals. From time to time, screams were heard; helmeted shadows went by the tent's red wall: now that Achilles had locked himself up with this dead man, the living appeared to him only as ghosts. A treacherous dampness rose from the bare ground; the footsteps of armies on the move shook the tent; its stakes wobbled in the shaky ground. Reconciled, the two sides struggled with the river of death: Achilles, pale, entered this Apocalyptic night. To him, the living were not precarious survivors of a still threatening wave of death; rather, it was the dead who seemed submerged in the vile deluge of the living. Against this moving, animated, formless water, Achilles defended the stones and the cement used to make tombs. When the fire coming from the forest of Mount Ida reached the port and licked the belly of ships, Achilles held against the trunks, the masts, the insolently fragile sails a flame that isn't afraid to kiss the dead on funeral pyres. Strange tribes from Asia emerged like rivers: caught up in Ajax's madness, Achilles slaughtered this cattle without recognizing its human traits. He was sending Patroclus herds for hunting parties in the otherworld. The Amazons appeared; a flood of breasts covered the slopes of the river; the army shook, aroused by that smell of bared fleece. All his life, Achilles had taken women to represent the instinctive part of misfortune, the one he did not choose but had to endure and couldn't accept. He blamed his mother for having made him a half-breed, halfway between a man and a god, therefore taking away from him half of the merit men earn in becoming gods. He bore her a grudge for having dipped him as a child in the Styx to immunize him against fear, as if heroism weren't

precisely a question of being vulnerable. He re-
sented Lycomedes' daughters not recognizing in
his travesty the opposite of disguise. He did not
forgive Briseis the humiliation of having loved
her. His blade sank in this pink froth, cutting
visceral Gordian knots: howling, giving birth to
death through the gaps in their wounds, the women
were entangled in the disheveling of their entrails
like horses in bullfight arenas. Penthesilea broke
loose from this heap of trampled women. She had
lowered her visor so that no one could be moved
by looking at her eyes; she alone dared give up the
advantage of fighting nude. Carapaced, helmeted,
masked in gold, this mineral Fury kept only her
hair and her voice as human attributes, but her
hair was golden and gold ran in this pure voice.
She was the only one among her companions who
had consented to have one of her breasts cut off,
but the mutilation was hardly noticeable on this
godlike chest. The dead women were dragged out
of the arena by their hair; the soldiers formed a
line transforming the battlefield into an arena,
pushing Achilles in the middle of a circle from
which murder would be his only way out. In this
khaki, field-gray, horizon-blue setting, the Ama-

zon's armor changed forms with each ensuing century, changed tint depending on the spotlights. With this Slavic woman making a dance step of each feint, the hand-to-hand combat became a tournament, then a Russian ballet. Invaded by the love found at the heart of hatred, Achilles moved forward, then back, riveted to this metal housing a victim. As though to break the spell, he threw his blade with all his might, pierced the thin breast-plate that had put god knew what pure soldier between him and this woman. Yielding, Penthesilea fell, unable to resist the iron rape. Orderlies rushed forward; the sputtering of flashbulbs going off sounded like machine-gun fire; impatient hands were skinning the golden corpse. Lifted, the visor revealed, instead of a face, a mask with blind eyes no longer responsive to kisses. Achilles was sobbing, holding up the head of this victim worthy of being a friend. She was the only creature in the world who looked like Patroclus.

To give yourself no more is to give yourself still, for you are giving your sacrifice.

Nothing dirtier than the ego.

The madman's crime is to prefer himself. I find this impious preference repulsive in those who kill and terrifying in those who love. To these misers, the creature loved is nothing more than a gold coin to clutch in your hands. He is only a god; he is hardly anything. I won't allow myself to turn you into an object, even into the Beloved Object.

The only horror is not to be used. Turn me into whatever you want, even a screen, even a metallic conductor.

You could fall suddenly into the void the dead go to: I would be comforted if you would bequeath me your hands. Only your hands would continue to exist, detached from you, unexplainable like those of marble gods turned into the dust and the limestone of their own tomb. They would survive your actions, the wretched bodies they caressed. They would no longer serve as intermediaries between you and things: they themselves would be changed into things. Innocent again now, since you would no longer be there to turn them into your accomplices, sad like greyhounds without masters, disconcerted like archangels to whom no god gives orders, your useless hands would rest on the lap of darkness. Your open hands incapable of giving or taking the slightest joy would have let me slump like a broken doll. I kiss the wrists of these indifferent hands you will no longer pull away from mine: I stroke the blue artery, the blood column that once spurted continuously like a fountain from the ground of your heart. With little sobs of contentment, I rest my head like a child between these palms filled with the stars, the crosses, the precipices of my previous fate.

I do not fear ghosts. The living are terrifying only because they have bodies.

There is no sterile love. No precaution can avert it. When I leave you, I have deep within me my suffering like a sort of terrible offspring.

ANTIGONE

OR THE CHOICE

―――――

W hat does this abysmal noon mean? Hatred weighs on Thebes like a horrible sun. Since the death of the Sphinx, nothing's secret in the vile city: everything comes to light. Like insipid water settling deep into wells, shadows shrink to the bottom of houses, to the feet of trees: rooms are no longer dark and cool. Strollers look like sleepwalkers in an endless white night. Jocasta strangled herself to stop seeing the sun. People sleep in broad daylight; people make love in broad daylight. Lying in the open air, the bodies of sleepers are like corpses of suicides; lovers are like dogs mating under the sun. Hearts are as dry as scorched fields; the new king's heart is dry as rock. So much drought calls for blood. Hatred infects souls; the sun's rays eat away at people's consciences, but their cancer remains. Oedipus lost his sight by

handling these dark rays. Only Antigone with-
stands these arrows shot by Apollo, as though grief
shielded her like sunglasses. She leaves this clay
city where hardened faces are molded like those on
tombstones; she goes with Oedipus through yawn-
ing doors that seem to vomit him out. She leads
along the roads of exile this father who is at the
same time her tragic older brother: he blesses the
fortunate offense that led him to Jocasta, as if
incest with the mother had been but the means
to beget himself a sister. She will have no peace
until she sees him rest in a night more absolute
than blindness, asleep in the bed of the Furies,
who will thereupon be transformed into shelter-
ing goddesses, since all suffering yielded to changes
into serenity. She refuses clothes, fresh linen, a
seat on the public carriage going to Thebes, things
which Theseus offers her as token charity. She
reaches, on foot, the city that has turned into crime
what was only a disaster, into exile what was only
a parting, into punishment what was only her fate.
Uncombed, sweating, object of derision to fools,
object of scandal to wise men, she follows the army
tracks in the open country littered with empty bot-
tles, heel-less shoes, and the abandoned sick already

taken for dead by the birds of prey. She heads
toward Thebes like Saint Peter returning to Rome
to be crucified. She slips through the seven circles
of armies camping around Thebes, invisible as a
lamp amid the fires of Hell. She enters by a secret
door in ramparts topped with the heads of victims
like those of Chinese cities; she sneaks through
streets emptied by the plague of hatred and shaken
in their foundations by the passage of tanks; she
climbs up to the platforms where wives and daughters howl in fierce joy at each shot that misses one
of their men; her face, bloodless between its long
black braids, appears in the battlements along the
rows of severed heads. She will not choose between
her warring brothers, as she will not choose between the opened chest and the dripping hands of
a man killing himself; the twins are but one single
wince of grief to her, as they were, at first, but one
single joyous spring in Jocasta's belly. She awaits
the outcome to devote herself to the loser, as if
defeat proved the justice of the cause. She goes
back down, drawn by the weight of her heart toward the swamps of the battlefield; she walks on
the dead like Jesus on the waters. Among the men
made equal by the appearance of decay, she recog-

nizes Polynices by his nakedness, which removed him from all deceit, and by the solitude surrounding him like an honor guard. She turns her back on the vile absolution that comes from punishing. When still alive, Eteocles, impaled by his success, was already mummified by the imposture of fame. But dead, Polynices exists as grief exists. He no longer runs the risk of ending up blind like Oedipus, of conquering like Eteocles, of ruling like Creon: he cannot gel; he can only rot. Beaten, stripped, dead, he has reached the bottom of human suffering: nothing comes between brother and sister, not even a virtue, not even a point of honor. Innocent of laws, scandalous from the cradle on, wrapped by crime as though by one common membrane, they share the terrible virginity of not being of this world; their two solitudes meet exactly as two mouths in a kiss. She bends over him like the sky over the earth, and with that gesture defines her universe; a dark possessive instinct makes her lean toward this culprit no one will claim from her. This dead man is the empty urn in which to pour all the wine of a great love. Her slim arms painfully lift this corpse contended for by vultures; she carries him, her crucified victim, as though carrying a cross. From the top of the ramparts, Creon sees this dead man coming held up by his immortal soul. Praetorians dash forward, wanting to drag this benevolent ghoul out of the cemetery. Their hands, ripping a seamless tunic on Antigone's shoulders, seize the corpse, which is already disintegrating, dissolving like a memory. Relieved of her dead weight, head bent, this girl seems to bear God. Creon sees red as though her bloodied rags were a flag. The pitiless city does not know twilights: day darkens all at once as when a lightbulb burns out: were the king to lift his eyes, the lighted streetlamps of Thebes would now shield from him the laws written in the sky. Men have no destiny when the world has no stars. Only Antigone, victim of divine law, was given as prerogative the obligation to perish and this privilege can explain the hatred against her. She moves forward, into this night shot through by searchlights. Her madwoman's hair, her beggar's rags, her broken, scavenger's fingernails show how far a sister's charity must go. In broad sunlight, she was pure water on soiled hands, shade inside a cask, kerchief on mouths of the deceased. At night, she becomes a lamp. Her devotion to Oedipus' punctured eyes shines on millions of blind men; her passion for her putrefied brother warms myriads of dead. Light can't be killed; it can only be suffocated: Antigone's suffering is hidden under the bushel. Creon throws it back to the gutter, to the catacombs. She returns to the source of origins, of treasures, of germination. She rejects Ismene, who is only a sister of the flesh. She dismisses in Haemon the terrible possibility to beget winners. She leaves, seeking her star at the farthest reaches of human reason, a star that can only be reached by going through the grave. Haemon, converted to the cause of defeat, runs behind her in dark corridors: son of a blind, deluded man, he is the third facet of her tragic love. He arrives in time to see her prepare the complicated system of slings and pulleys that will allow her to escape to God. Abysmal noon spoke of fury; abysmal midnight speaks of despair. Time no longer exists in this Thebes deprived of stars; sleepers spread out in absolute darkness no longer see their conscience. Creon lying in Oedipus' bed rests on Reasons of State, a hard pillow. Drunk with justice, a few protestors scattered in the streets, stumbled in the night and sprawled at the foot of boundary stones.

Suddenly, in the stupefied silence of the city sleeping off its crime, an underground beating is heard,
grows louder, forces itself on Creon's insomnia,
becomes his nightmare. Creon gets up, feels his
way to the door of tunnels known only to him, dis-
covers in the underground clay the footprints of
his oldest son. A vague phosphorescence emanating
from Antigone reveals Haemon hanging from the
neck of the dead woman and carried along by the
swing of this pendulum that seems to measure
death's amplitude. They are tied one to the other
as if to make a heavier weight; their slow oscilla-
tion drives them each time further into the grave,
and this throbbing weight rewinds the machinery
of the stars. The revealing noise crosses the pave-
ments, the marble tiling, the clay walls, fills the
parched air with an arterial throb. The soothsayers
lie down, ear to the ground, listening, like doctors,
to the lethargic chest of the earth. Time starts running again to the sound of God's clock. The world's
pendulum is Antigone's heart.

Loving eyes closed is to love blindly. Loving eyes open is perhaps to love madly: to accept desperately. I love you to distraction.

I have an ignominious hope left. In spite of myself, I am banking on an instinctual continuity, the equivalent, in the life of the heart, of an absent-minded action mistaking a name, a door. Horrified at myself, I wish you Camille's betrayal, a failure with Claude, a scandal that would separate you from Hippolytus. Any faux pas could make you fall on my body.

One reaches all great events of life a virgin. I am afraid of not knowing how to deal with my suffering.

A god who wants me to live ordered you to stop loving me. I don't bear happiness well. Lack of habit. In your arms, I could only die.

Usefulness of love. Voluptuaries manage the exploration of pleasure without it. One doesn't know what to do with delirium while experimenting with the mingling and mixing of bodies. Then one realizes there are still discoveries to be made in a dark hemisphere. One needed love to learn suffering.

LENA

OR THE SECRET

L ena was Aristogiton's concubine and more his servant than his mistress. They lived in a cottage near Saint-Sôtir Chapel: she grew tender squash and abundant eggplants in the little garden, salted the anchovies, cut the red watermelon meat into quarters, took the laundry down to wash in the dry Ilissus River bed, saw to it that her master took a scarf with him so that he wouldn't catch cold after the workouts in the stadium. As reward for so much care, he let himself be loved. They went out together: they went to little cafés to listen to records of popular songs spinning plaintively and ardently like a dark sun. She was proud to see her picture in newspapers on the front page of the sports section. He had entered in the Olympic boxing matches; he had permitted her to come along; she bore the dust of the roads without complaining, the tiresome ambling of mules, the miserable inns where water was more expensive than their best island wine. The noise of cars on the road was so continuous that it even drowned out the squeaking sound of cicadas. One day, at noon, rounding a curve on a hill, she discovered under her feet the valley Olympia, hollow like the palm of a god carrying a statue of Victory in his hand. Heat vapors floated on altars, in kitchens, in the fair's little shops whose cheap jewelry Lena coveted. In order not to lose her master in the crowd, she had taken the fine edge of his coat between her teeth. She had rubbed grease on those idols kind enough not to repulse a servant's advances; she had decorated them with ribbons and smeared them with kisses. She had recited all the prayers she knew to ask for her master's success, and had yelled her repertoire of curses against his rivals. Separated from him during long abstinences imposed on athletes, she had slept alone under the tent, in the women's quarters, outside the enclosure reserved for the contestants; she had repulsed hands stretching in the dark, indifferent even to the sunflower-seed cornets proffered by her neighbors. The boxer's imagination was filled with oil-rubbed torsos and shaven, slippery heads: she had the im-

pression that Aristogiton neglected her for his adversaries; the evening of the Games, she had caught
sight of him carried triumphantly in the stadium
halls, panting like after lovemaking, caught by the
reporters' questions, by the photographers' cameras;
she had the impression that he cheated on her with
Fame. His life was now that of a champion and
was spent partying with society people; she had
seen him leave the ritual banquet accompanied by
a noble young Athenian, drunk with a drunken-
ness she hoped was due to alcohol, for one can be
cured of that addiction faster than that of happiness. He had returned to Athens in Harmodius'
car, leaving Lena to the care of one of her neighbors; he had disappeared in a cloud of dust, removed from her caresses like a dead man or a god;
the last image she had of him was that of a scarf
floating on a brown nape. Like an abandoned dog
following his master at a distance, she started, in
the opposite direction, the long way home; women
hurried through hills here, afraid of seeing satyrs
in deserted places. In each village inn where she
stopped to buy a bit of shade and a cup of coffee
flanked by a glass of water, she found the owner
still busy counting the gold coins negligently

dropped from the pockets of these two men; they had taken the best rooms everywhere, drank the best wines, forced the singers to bray until dawn; Lena's pride, which was still love, tended the wounds of her love, which was still pride. Little by little, the young kidnapping god stopped being only a face and became a name, a brief history. The mechanic from Patras told her that his name was Harmodius. Pyrgos' horse dealer talked of his racehorses, the Styx ferryman of the dead knew that he was an orphan and that his father had just landed on the other bank. The highwaymen were aware that the tyrant of Athens had heaped riches on him, Corinth's courtesans had heard that he was handsome. Everyone, even the beggars, even the village idiots, knew that he was bringing back the boxing champion of the Olympic Games in his sports car: this radiating boy was nothing more than the trophy, the vase decorated with streamers, the long-haired image of Victory. In Megara the tollbooth keeper informed Lena that Harmodius had refused to get out of the way of the Chief of State's carriage and that Hipparchus had violently berated the young man for his lack of gratitude, for keeping such plebian company: his militia had taken back, by force, the car that wasn't his, he said, to ride around in with a boxer. In the city of Athens, Lena shook at the sound of the seditious clamor echoing her master's name on ten thousand pairs of lips; in honor of the victor, young Athenians organized a torchlight parade that Hipparchus refused to attend: pine trees wrenched from the ground by their roots wept copiously their sacrificed resin. In the cottage near Saint-Sôtir, dancers hitting the paved courtyard ground unevenly with their heels cast a moving, naked fresco on the wall. So as not to disturb anyone, Lena sneaked in noiselessly through the kitchen door. The pots and pans no longer spoke a familiar language to her; clumsy hands had prepared a meal: she cut her finger picking up a piece of broken glass. She tried in vain, with stroking, caresses, and tidbits, to win over Harmodius' greyhound lying in the pantry. She expected her master to bring her the menus of his dinners in high society, but he does not even notice her smiles; to get rid of her, he sends her to his little farm in Decelea to help with the grape harvest. She foresees a marriage between her master and Harmodius' sister: she thinks with horror about a spouse, with anguish about their children.

She lives in the shadow of torches that the handsome Eros casts on weddings. The lack of an en-
gagement party only half reassures this innocent
who mistakes the danger: Harmodius has intro-
duced misfortune in this house like a veiled mistress: she feels forsaken for this impalpable woman.
One evening, a man in whose worn features she
does not recognize Hipparchus' effigy multiplied ad
infinitum on stamps and coins, knocks at the servants' door, shyly asking for the bread of truth.
Entering the room by chance, Aristogiton finds her
sitting at the table next to this suspicious beggar;
he mistrusts her too much to make a scene; she is
chased away from the room suddenly filled with
screams. A few days later, Harmodius finds his
friend lying by the spring Clepsydra: he had been
caught in an ambush. Harmodius calls Lena to
help him carry the boxer's body, tattooed with
knife wounds, to the only couch in the house:
their hands blackened by iodine meet on his
stabbed chest. Lena sees the typical wrinkle of
Apollo-the-healer on Harmodius' bent forehead.
She stretches her restless hands toward the young
man, begging him to save her master: she is not
surprised to hear him blame himself for each

wound as though he were responsible for them: it seems natural to her that a god be in turn both savior and murderer. The footsteps of a plainclothesman going back and forth on the deserted road makes the wounded man lying on the couch shudder; only Harmodius continues to venture downtown as if no knife could open a passage in his flesh, and to Lena this is additional proof that he is a god. The two men fear her tongue so much that they try to make her believe yesterday's assault happened during a drunken brawl, afraid perhaps that she could jeopardize their chances for revenge by talking with the corner butcher or groceryman. Lena is shocked to notice that they make the dog taste the stews she prepares them, as though she had good reason to hate them. To let things blow over, they go camping in Cretan fashion with some friends on the Parnes; they keep from her the location of the cave they sleep in; she is entrusted with bringing them food, which she deposits under a stone as though intended to appease the dead roaming around the living. As an offering, she brings Aristogiton black wine and quarters of bleeding meat, but she can't make this livid specter, who no longer kisses her, speak. This somnambulist is already a dead man sleepwalking toward his grave, like Jewish corpses pilgrimaging to Josaphat. Shyly she touches his knees, his naked feet, to be sure they are still warm; she thinks she sees in Harmodius' hands the dowsing stick of Hermes, leader of souls. Their return to Athens takes place between the dogs of fear and the wolves of revenge: grotesque figures of penniless squires, caseless lawyers, discontented soldiers slip into the room like shadows carried by the presence of a god. Since Harmodius, taking precautions, no longer sleeps at home, Lena, relegated to the attic, can't sit anymore with her master as one sits with a patient, can't tuck him in every night as one tucks in a child. Hidden on the terrace, she watches the untiring opening and closing of this house stricken with insomnia: not understanding anything, she is nevertheless there during these comings and goings that shuttle back and forth weaving revenge. She is made to sew looped crosses on brown wool uniforms for an upcoming sports event. Lamps are burning on all Athenian rooftops that evening: noble maidens prepare their white communicant robes for tomorrow's procession: deep within the sanctuary, the Holy Virgin's red hair is washed and set; a million incense grains smoke under Athena's nose. Lena holds on her lap young Irini, who now lives with them because Harmodius is afraid that Hipparchus might get even with him by kidnapping his little sister. As though both their hopes had been betrayed, she feels full of pity for this child who she once feared would enter the house crowned as a bride. She spends the night sorting out red roses that the little girl will throw by the handful on the passage of the Very Holy Virgin: Harmodius plunges his impatient hands in the basket; they seem drenched with blood. At the hour that the Athens sky becomes pearly, Lena takes Irini by the hand and climbs the ramps of the Propylaea; the little girl is quivering in the luster of her veils . . . Ten thousand candle flames shine feebly in the early-morning light like so many will-o'-the-wisps that did not have time to go back into their graves. Hipparchus, still drunk on nightmares, blinks before all this whiteness, absentmindedly examines the blue and white procession of Athena's Daughters. Suddenly a haunted resemblance grazes the formless face of little Irini for him: the tyrant, seized with frenzy, shakes the arm of the young

thief who dares to steal her brother's eyes, screams
that the sister of the wretch poisoning his dreams
be chased away far from his sight. The child falls
on her knees; upset, the basket spills its red con-
tents: tears muddle the resemblance on the little
girl's face. At the hour the sky is gold like this
inalterable heart, Lena brings home the tousled
child stripped of her basket: Harmodius bursts
with joy, learning of this wished-for affront. Lena,
kneeling on the courtyard pavement, head wagging
like that of a professional mourner, feels on her
forehead the hand of this hard youth who looks like
a Nemesis: the tyrant's insults, his threats, which
she repeats, not trying to understand them, take
on in her dull voice the horrible platitude of irre-
vocable verdicts and tired truths. Each insult adds
on Harmodius' face a frown or a scornful smile;
in the presence of this god who didn't even bother
to find out her name, Lena enjoys being alive,
being useful, perhaps even being able to cause
suffering. She helps Harmodius mutilate the beautiful laurel trees of the courtyard as though the first
task consisted in eliminating all shade: she leaves
the garden with the two men, hiding broad kitchen
knives among sheaves of flowers: she closes the

door on Irini taking her siesta, on the dove cage, on the cardboard box the cicadas graze in, on the past bottomless as a dream now. The crowds, dressed in their Sunday best, separate her from her masters; she no longer distinguishes between them. She sets out on their tracks along the construction sites of the Parthenon, stumbling on the piles of half-polished rocks that make the Temple of the Virgin look like its future ruins. As the sun sets, she sees the two friends disappear behind columns that look like machines to extract gods from human hearts. Screams, bombs explode: disemboweled, Hipparchus' older brother lies on the altar covered with blood and glowing embers; he seems to be offering his entrails to the priests to be read: leaning against a column so as not to fall, Hipparchus, mortally wounded, keeps on screaming orders. The Propylaea doors are shut to bar the rebels from the only opening that doesn't look out on a precipice. Caught in this marble and sky trap, running helter-skelter, the conspirators stumble on piles of gods. Wounded in the leg, Aristogiton is captured by policemen at the bottom of Pan's grottoes. The lynched body of Harmodius is dismembered by the crowd like that of Bacchus during bloody rites: foes, or perhaps friends, pass from hand to hand this terrifying relic. Lena kneels, gathers Harmodius' hair in her apron as though this were the most pressing service she could render her master. Bloodhounds jump on her. When her hands are tied, they no longer look like household utensils; they become martyr's hands, angelic knuckles. She climbs into the police van like the dead climbing into the fateful barque. She crosses a stagnant Athens, a city frozen by fear where faces hide behind closed shutters lest they should have to judge. She alights in front of a house whose hospital and prisonlike aspect shows that it is the Chief of State's palace. In the main entrance, she runs into Aristogiton stumbling on his wounded legs: she lets the firing squad go by without lifting her eyes to her master; they are already glazed like the pupils of the dead. The cracking noise of gunfire coming from the next courtyard rings for her like a salvo over Harmodius' grave. She is shoved into a whitewashed room where tortured people look like dying animals and the executioners like vivisectionists. Hipparchus, lying on a stretcher, turns his bandaged head toward her, gropes for her hands clutched on the only truth he still hungers for, speaks to her so softly and so close to her ear that the interrogation seems like the whispering of an amorous confidence. He demands names, confessions. What did she see? Who were their accomplices? Did the eldest of the two lead the younger one into this death race? Was the boxer only dealing Harmodius' blows? Did he know that the master did not hate him, would have forgiven? Did he often speak of him? Was he sad? A desperate intimacy is starting up between this man and woman possessed by the same god, dying of the same malady, and whose lackluster glances turn toward two absences. Under this interrogation, Lena clenches her teeth, pinches her lips. Her masters would stop talking when she came into the room to pass them the plates of food; she stayed on the threshold of their lives like a dog lying by the door. Devoid of memories, this woman strives through pride to make them believe that she knows everything, that her masters entrusted her their hearts, knowing she was reliable, and that she can spit out their past if she chooses to. She is stretched out on the rack so that the executioners can operate on her silence. She, so flamelike, is threatened with water torture; she, so pure and humble, is threatened with fire torture. She fears the pain that will wrench from her only the humiliating confession that she was just a servant and not an accomplice. As though heaved up by her lungs, a jet of blood spurts from her mouth. She has cut off her tongue to keep from revealing the secrets she doesn't have.

---

*"Burned with more fires . . ." Worn-out beast . . .
a hot whip lashes my back. I rediscovered the true
meaning of the poetic metaphors. I wake up each
night with my own blood ablaze.*

*I have known nothing but adoration or debauchery.
Which is saying what? I have known nothing but
adoration or pity.*

*Christians pray before a cross, press it to their lips.
This piece of wood satisfies them even if no Saviour hangs on it. The respect due martyred victims ends up ennobling the vile instrument of torture: you don't love people enough if you don't
worship their misery, their debasement, their misfortune.*

When I lose everything, I still have God left. If I misplace God, I find you again. You can't have both at once, the immense night and the sun.

Jacob was wrestling with the angel in the land of Gilead. This angel is God, since his adversary came out of that struggle licked, hip dislocated by defeat. The steps of the golden staircase are only for those who first accept this eternal undoing. God is everything that exceeds us, that got the better of us. Death is God, and the world, and the idea of God for the weak wrestler who lets himself be thrown by their huge wingbeats. You are God: you could break me.

I will not fall. I have reached the center. I listen to the striking of who knows what divine clock through the thin carnal wall of a life full of blood, of shudderings, and of breathings. I am near the mysterious kernel of things as one is sometimes near a heart at night.

MARY MAGDALENE

OR SALVATION

My name is Mary: people call me Mary Magdalene. Magdalene is the name of my village; my mother owned fields there and my father owned vineyards. I come from Magdala. At noon, my sister Martha would bring pitchers of beer to the farm workers; but me, I went to them empty-handed; they lapped up my smile; their eyes went over me as though I were an almost ripe fruit which needs only a little more sun to be full-flavored. My eyes were two panthers caught in the net of my lashes; my mouth, almost black, looked like a swollen bloodsucker. Our dovecote was full of doves, the bread bin of bread, our coffins of money stamped with Caesar's effigy. Martha was wearing out her eyes marking my trousseau with John's initials. John's mother owned fisheries; John's father owned vineyards. Seated, on our wedding day, under the fountain's fig tree, John and I were already feeling the intolerable weight of seventy years of happiness pressing on us. The same dance tunes would be played at our daughters' weddings; I felt heavy with the children they would bear. John came to me from the bottom of his childhood; he seemed to smile to invisible angels, they being his sole companions; I had rejected a Roman centurion's proposition for him. He fled the taverns where prostitutes sway like vipers to the exciting sounds of a sad flute; he averted his eyes from the round faces of farm girls. Loving his innocence was my first sin. I didn't know that I fought against an invisible rival as had done our father Jacob against the Angel, and that what was at stake in the struggle was this boy in whose disheveled hair a halo was already outlined by bits of straw. I didn't know that someone else had loved John before my loving him, before his loving himself; I didn't know that God is the last resort of loners. I was presiding over the wedding banquet in the women's quarters; matrons were whispering procurers' secrets in my ears, courtesan tricks; the flute was screaming like a virgin, struck drums were beating like hearts; women sprawled in the shadows, in bundles of veils, bunches of breasts, were begrudging me in a dull voice the violent happiness of receiving the Bridegroom. In the yard, stuck sheep wailed like the innocent in the hands of Herod's butchers; I didn't hear the bleating of the Ravishing Lamb in the distance. Evening fumes were blurring everything in the high room. The twilight concealed the sense of forms and the color of things; I did not notice, seated among the poor relatives at the end of the men's table, the white vagabond who with a touch, with a kiss, was transmitting a terrible leprosy to young men, the sort of illness that would force them to withdraw from everything. I did not guess the presence of the Seducer who makes renunciation as sweet as sin. Doors were shut; perfumes were burned to ward off devils; we were left alone. Lifting my eyes, I saw that John had moved through his wedding feast like someone crossing a square filled with people for a public celebration. His trembling was only from sorrow, his pallor only from shame, his fear only for failing to possess God. I could not tell on John's face the grimace of disgust from that of desire; I was a virgin, and

besides, any woman in love is only a poor innocent. It's only later that I understood that for him
I represented the worst corporal offense, the legitimate sin, approved by custom, so much more
dangerous since it incurs no condemnation. He
had chosen me, the most veiled of maidens, to
court while secretly hoping not to succeed; I ac-
counted for his distaste of readily available prey;
sitting on the bed, I was nothing more now than
an easy woman. His impotency gave us a stronger
bond than sexual hunger, which is so often used
to justify love: both of us wanted to yield to a
will more forceful than ours, to give ourselves,
to be taken: we would bear every conceivable
pain to beget a new life. This soul, under the
guise of a young man, was running toward a
Bridegroom. He was leaning against a windowpane gradually tarnished by his breath. The stars'
weary eyes were not even spying on us anymore:
a servant on the lookout on the other side of the
threshold mistook my sobs perhaps for gasps of
love. A voice rising in the night called out for
John three times, as it happens in front of houses
where someone is going to die; John opened the
window, leaned forward to gauge the shadows'

depth, saw God. I saw only darkness, that is to say, His coat. John tore the sheets from the bed and tied them together to make a rope: fireflies were blinking like stars on the ground, so that he seemed to sink into the sky. I lost sight of this deserter who preferred to lie on God's bosom rather than a woman's. Carefully, I opened the door of the room where only a leave-taking had occurred; I stepped over the guests snoring in the entrance hall, I took Lazarus' hood from the coatrack. The night was too dark to look for the mark of divine footprints on the ground; the cobblestones I tripped on were not those I had hopped over coming home from school; for the first time I saw the houses from the outside, as those who have no homes see them. In evil-looking alleys, obscene suggestions oozed out of toothless pimps and procuresses, drunkards' vomit under the arcades of the market recalled the wine puddles of the wedding feast. To escape the watch, I ran along the wooden galleries of the inn to the Roman lieutenant's room. This ruffian opened the door for me still drunk from all the toasts quaffed in my honor at Lazarus' table; he took me for one of the sluts he was in the habit of sleeping with. I kept my face hidden in my black wool hood; I was less shy with my body: when he recognized me, I was already Mary Magdalene. I did not tell him that John had abandoned me on my wedding night, lest he feel compelled to pour the insipid water of his pity into the wine of his desire. I let him believe that I chose his hairy arms over the long, always joined hands of my pale fiancé. I kept John's fugue with God as his secret. The children of the village found out where I was; they threw stones at me. Lazarus had the millpond dredged, thinking to fish out John's corpse: Martha lowered her head when she walked by the inn; John's mother asked me to answer for the alleged suicide of her only son; I did not speak up in my defense, finding it less humiliating to have them all think the runaway had loved me madly. The following month, Marius was transferred to Gaza to the Palestine second division; I couldn't scrape up enough money to buy a third-class seat in those carriages reserved since time immemorial for prophets, for the poor, for soldiers on leave, for Messiahs. The innkeeper kept me on to wipe glasses; I learned the tricks of the trade from my boss. It was sweet to me that the woman scorned by John would fall abruptly to the lowest of the lowest: to me, each blow, each kiss molded a face, breasts, a body very different from the one John hadn't caressed. A Bedouin camel-driver agreed to take me to Jaffa as payment in kind: a captain from Marseilles took me on his boat; lying in the stern, I let myself be caught in the warm trembling of the foaming sea. In a bar in Piraeus, a Greek philosopher taught me wisdom as one more debauchery. In Smyrna, the generosity of a banker showed me how pearls, oyster cankers, and tiger furs can soften the skin of a naked woman, so that I was envied while being coveted. In Jerusalem a Pharisee got me into the habit of using hypocrisy as a makeup that never fails. In a hovel in Caesarea, a cured paraplegic told me about God. In spite of Angels trying to lead him back to the heavens, God kept on prowling from village to village, scoffing at the priests, insulting the rich, sowing discord in families, excusing the adulteress, practicing his scandalous Messiah profession everywhere. Even eternity can become a fad for a while; to one of those Tuesdays where only famous people were invited, Simon the Pharisee had the idea to ask God to come. I had been sleeping around only to give this Friend a less naïve rival: to seduce God was to take from John his eternal support; it was to force him to fall back on me with all the weight of his body. We sin because God is not: it's because nothing perfect is set before our eyes that we settle for human beings. As soon as John would understand that God is only a man, all reason not to prefer my breasts to Him would vanish. I got decked out as though for a ball; I got perfumed as though for bed. At my entrance in the banquet hall, all jaws dropped: the Apostles rose in an uproar so that they would not be contaminated by the grazing of my skirt: in the eyes of these upstanding citizens I was impure, as though I were continuously menstruating. Only God did not rise from his leather bench; instinctively I recognized these feet worn down to the bone by having walked on all roads of our Hell, this hair infected by a vermin of stars, these huge eyes pure as the last pieces of the sky he had left. He was ugly as suffering: he was dirty as sin. Choking back my spit, I fell on my knees, incapable of adding sarcasm to the terrible weight of God's anguish. I saw at once that I would not be able to seduce him, since he did not run from me. I undid my hair so as to better cover up my sin; I emptied before him the flask of my memories. I understood that this outlawed God must have slipped

out one morning through dawn's doors, leaving
behind him the Trinity surprised at being only a
twosome. He had settled down here in the com-
monplace of time; he lavished himself on countless
people passing by who refused him their soul but
who demanded every tangible joy. He bore the
company of highwaymen, the contact of lepers, the
insolence of policemen: like me, he agreed to the
terrible lot of belonging to all. He placed on my
head his large cadaverous hand, which seemed already emptied of blood: all we ever do is change
enslavements: at the exact moment the devils left
me, I became possessed by God. John was erased
from my life as though the Evangelist had been
only the Precursor for me: placed in front of the
Passion, I forgot love. I accepted purity like a worse
perversion: I spent sleepless nights, shivering with
dew and tears, lying outdoors in the fields among
the Apostles, a bunch of soaked sheep in love with
the Shepherd. I envied the dead the prophets lay
down on to raise them. I helped the divine bone-
setter with his magic cures: I rubbed mud in the
eyes of those born blind. I let Martha toil in my
stead that day of Bethany's dinner, lest John sit by
the celestial knees on the stool I would have left.

My tears, my cries earned from this kind miracle
worker the second birth of Lazarus: this dead man
swaddled in his shroud taking his first steps on the
threshold of his grave was almost our common
child. I recruited disciples for him; I dunked my
pale hands into the dishwater of the Last Supper;
I kept watch on the square of the Olive Trees while
the business of the Redemption was taking place. I
loved him so much that I stopped pitying him; my
love took care to increase the anguish that made
him God. So as not to ruin his career as Saviour, I
consented to see him die as a mistress consents to
the rich marriage of the man she loves: in the Hall
of the Tribunal, when Pilate gave us the choice between a thief and God, I screamed like the others
in favor of Barabbas. I saw Him lie down on the
vertical bed of his eternal wedlock: I witnessed the
horrible binding of ropes, the kiss of the sponge
still soaked with a marine bitterness, the blow of
the soldier's lance trying to pierce the heart of this
sublime vampire so that he not rise to suck our
whole future. I felt on my forehead the shudder of
this gentle owl nailed to the door of Time. A wind
of death was digging into a sky slashed like a sail;
dragged by the weight of the Cross, the world

leaned to the side of evening. The pale captain hung from the yard of the three-masted ship submerged by Sin: the carpenter's son atoned for the mistakes of his Holy Father. I knew nothing good would come of his torment: the only result of this execution would be to teach men they can get rid of God. The divine convict would scatter on earth only useless seeds of blood. The loaded dice of Chance were tossed in vain in sentinels' hands; what was left of the infinite Robe would not be enough for anyone to make himself a garment. In vain did I pour on his feet the flood of my bleached hair; in vain did I try to comfort the only mother to conceive God. My woman and she-wolf screams did not reach my dead master. The thieves, at least, shared the same end: at the foot of the axis through which the grief of the whole world passed, I succeeded only in interrupting His dialogue with Dismas, the highwayman. Ladders were raised, ropes were hauled. God was plucked like a fruit ripe and ready to rot in the ground of graveyards. For the first time, his inert head took my shoulder: our hands were coated red from the juice of his heart, sticky as they are during the grape harvest. Joseph of Arimathea went ahead carrying a lantern;

John and I followed, buckling under the weight of this body heavier than the man; some soldiers helped us block the opening of the tomb with a millstone. In the coolness of sunset, we went back to town, dazed to run into the shops again, the theaters, the insolence of waiters in public houses, the evening papers that had treated the Passion as just another news item. I spent the night choosing among my most handsome courtesan bed sheets. At daybreak I sent Martha out to buy all we could afford of perfume. Roosters crooned as though striving to revive Peter's repentance: surprised to see that daylight was here, I followed a suburban road where apple trees recalled Original Sin and vineyards Redemption. Even though the wind came from the north, you couldn't detect the odor of God's corpse. Guided by a memory, an incorruptible angel, I was going down a pit dug into the deepest part of myself; I was approaching this body as though it were my own grave. I had given up all hopes of Easter, all promises of resurrection. I did not notice that the millstone was split lengthwise from some divine fermentation: God had risen from death as though leaving a sleepless bed; the sheets begged from the gardener were hanging from the

74

unmade tomb. For the second time in my life, I was standing in front of a deserted bed. Incense grains rolling on the sepulcher ground fell deeply into the night. The walls reverberated with my unappeased ghoulish howls; being beside myself, I hit the lintel stone with my forehead. Outside, the narcissus had stayed intact, like snow unmarked by any human trace: those who had just kidnapped God had walked on the sky. Leaning over the ground, the gardener was weeding a flower bed: he lifted his head from under a big straw hat that seemed a halo of sun and summer; I fell on my knees, seized by the sweet trembling of a woman in love who feels the substance of her heart spreading through her body. The man had on his shoulder the rake he uses to erase our sins: he held in his hands the ball of thread and the shears the Fates had entrusted to their eternal brother. Perhaps he was getting ready to go down to the underworld by way of the roots. He knew the nettles' secret remorse, the worms' agony: the pallor of death had not left him, so that he looked disguised into a lily of the field. I thought that his first move would be to push back this sinner contaminated by desire. I was a slug in this flowery universe. The air was so cool that the upturned palms of my hands felt as though they were pushing against glass: my dead master had gone through the mirror of Time to the other side. The steam of my breath clouded over the great image: God was erased like a reflection disappearing from this windowpane of dawn. My opaque body was no obstacle for the Resurrected Man. A cracking noise was heard; it might have been coming from the deepest part of me: I fell spread-eagled, dragged by the weight of my heart: there was nothing behind the glass I had just broken. Once again, I was emptier than a widow, lonelier than an abandoned woman. I understood at last the full meaning of God's atrocity. God had not only stolen a creature's love from me at an age when one deems them irreplaceable, but he had also long ago taken from me my morning sicknesses, the sleep that would follow giving birth, the old-woman naps that would be mine on the village square, the tomb at the bottom of the enclosure where my children would have laid me. After my innocence, God had withdrawn my sins: when I was just starting out as a courtesan, he removed my chances to go on the stage or to seduce Caesar. After his corpse, he took his ghost from me: he didn't even let me get drunk on an illusion. Like the most jealous of lovers, he destroyed this beauty that could have led to backslides into beds of desire. My breasts hang; I look like God's old mistress, Death. Like the worst maniac, he loved my tears only. But this God who took everything from me did not give me much. I got only a crumb of the infinite love: like a first-comer, I shared his heart with everyone. My former lovers lay on my body without worrying about my soul; my celestial friend took care only to warm my eternal soul, so that half of me never stopped suffering. And yet he saved me. Thanks to him, I had only the unhappy part of joys, the only one that is inexhaustible. I escape the routines of housework and bed, the dead weight of money, the impasse of success, the satisfaction of honor, the charms of infamy. Since the man sentenced to Mary Magdalene's love escaped to the sky, I avoid the insipid mistake of being necessary to God. I did right in letting the great divine wave spin me: I don't regret being refashioned by the Lord's hands. He saved me neither from death nor from harm nor from crime, since it's through them that one is saved. He saved me from happiness.

When I see you again, everything becomes limpid again. I am willing to suffer.

And you are going? You are going? . . . No, you are not going: I am keeping you . . . You leave your soul, like a coat, in my hands.

Love one another? No, you are not another. I pity you as I pity myself.

I have known young men who came from the world of gods. Their gestures made one think of star crossings; one wasn't surprised to find their tough porphyry heart insensitive; if they stretched out their palms in begging, their exquisite rapaciousness was a godly vice. Like all gods, they evoked disturbing kinships with wolves, jackals, and vipers: guillotined, they would have looked like pale de-

capitated statues. Some women, young girls, come from the world of Madonnas: the worst of them nurse hope like a child destined to future crucifixions. Some of my friends come from the world of wise men, from a sort of India or an inner China: the world around them vanishes like smoke; near these cold ponds reflecting the image of things, nightmares prowl like tamed tigers. Eros, my hard idol, your arms stretched toward me are wing vertebrae. I made you my Virtue; I accept seeing in you a Domination, a Power. I entrust myself to this terrible airplane propelled by a heart. At night, when we are drifting in slums together, your nude body seems then an Angel told to watch over your soul.

My God, I place my body between your hands again.

We say: mad with joy. We should say: wise with grief.

To possess is the same thing as to know: the Bible is always right. Love is a sorcerer: it knows the secrets; love is a dowser: it knows the sources. In-

difference is one-eyed; hate is blind; side by side they stumble into the pit of disdain. Indifference is ignorant; love knows; it spells out the flesh. You must have pleasure from a creature to contemplate him naked. I had to love you to understand that the most mediocre or the worst of human beings is worthy, up there, of inspiring God's eternal sacrifice.

Six days ago, six months ago, it will be six years, it will have been six centuries . . . Ah, to die in order to stop Time.

PHAEDO

OR THE DANCE

L isten, Cebes . . . I am whispering because it's only when we whisper that we really listen to ourselves. I am going to die, Cebes. Don't shake your head, don't say that you know, that we are all going to die. Time doesn't cost you philosophers anything: yet Time exists, since it sweetens us like fruit and dries us like grass. For those in love, time disappeared, since lovers tore out their hearts to give them to those they love; and that is why they are insensitive to thousands of men and women who are not part of their love, and that's why they safely weep and despair. And that's why those who are loved gauge old age and death by the slowing down of these hearts, timekeepers of the blood. For those who suffer, time does not exist; time has been in such a rush that it has destroyed itself, since each hour of torment is like a storm that lasts a hundred years. Each time I suffered, I

would smile to get a smile in return, and grief became the radiant face of a woman, all the more
beautiful because you had not noticed her beauty
before. I know of grief what its opposite teaches,
as in the same way life gave me the little enlighten-
ment I already hold from death. Like Narcissus in
his spring, I have looked at myself in the mirrors of
human eyes: the image they reflected was so radiant
that I was grateful to myself for bringing so much
happiness. I know of love what little the eyes of
those who love me taught me. Long ago in Elis,
surrounded by a hint of fame, I measured the pro-
gression of my adolescence by the smiles gradually
more and more trembling around me. Lying down
on the past of my race as if it were a fertile ground,
I was covered by my wealth as by a golden blanket.
Stars revolved like beacons; flowers became fruit,
the dunghill flowered; couples walked by like pairs
of convicts or village newlyweds; the fife of desire
and the drum of death set their sad waltz in motion;
it never lacked dancers. The road they thought
straight seemed circular to the adolescent lying in
the center of the future. My hair was blowing in
the wind, my eyelashes seemed to keep my eyes
prisoner of my eyelids; my blood flowed in a

thousand detours like underground streams, black
to the eyes of nocturnal shades but scarlet in the
sun, should the sun ever rise on the kingdom of
the dead. My penis moved like a bird looking for
a dark nest. I grew, bursting space, shattering it
into blue pieces of bark around me. I stood up;
rebuffed by school walls, my hands stretched out
in the dark, seeking to gather Omens; movement
started in me like a divine gravitation, the spring
rain ran down my bare trunk. The soles of my feet
remained my only contact with the fatal ground
that would someday take me back . . . Drunk with
life, dizzy with hope, in order not to fall I grabbed
hold of the smooth sweet shoulders of playmates
chancing to walk by; we fell together and it was
this tussle that we called love. My tender friends
were for me only targets I felt I had to strike at the
heart; they were colts to be stroked by a slow-motion
caress on the neck until the red tissue of blood
showed under the skin's pale silk. And the most
handsome ones, Cebes, were only a prize or victory
booty, a sweet proffered cup in which to pour your
whole life. Others were hedges, obstacles, hidden
trenches behind bunches of green brushwood
sticks. I left for the Olympics in the custody of a

blind pedagogue; I won first prize in the children's competition. The golden threads of ribbons, suddenly invisible, were lost in my hair. My hand threw the disk; its momentum drew the pure curve of a wing between the goal and me. Ten thousand chests gasped at the movement of my naked arm. At night, sleeping on the paternal roof, I watched the stars turning in an Olympic stadium covered with dark sand, but I did not try to read the future. The days awaiting me seemed filled with fighters' hugs, friendly fist blows, horses galloping toward who knew what happiness. Suddenly a clamor broke out under the walls of my native city; a veil of smoke covered the face of the sky. Columns of fire replaced columns of stone. The din of dishes breaking in the kitchen covered up the screams of servant girls being raped; a broken lyre moaned like a virgin in the arms of a drunken man. My family disappeared among ruins smeared with blood. The world tottered, fell, and was annihilated without my knowing if it was a genuine siege, a true blaze, a real massacre, or if these enemies were only lovers and if what caught fire was nothing but my heart. Pale, naked, my shame reflected in golden shields, I was grateful to these dashing adversaries for trampling my past. Everything ended in scenes of whipping and enslavement; that too, Cebes, is one of the consequences of love. Looking for gain, tradesmen flocked to the city that had been taken by storm. I was standing on the public square: the world with its meadows, its hills where my dogs would no longer pursue stags, its groves bursting with fruit that were no longer mine, its purple silky waves I would no longer indolently sail on, all spun around me like a gigantic torture wheel on which I was stretched. The dusty market air was a single pile of arms, legs, breasts probed by the steel of lances; blood and sweat ran down my face that seemed to smile because the sun made me grimace. Dark crusts of flies stuck to our burns. The unbearable heat of the ground forced me to lift my bare feet, one after the other, so that by sheer horror I seemed to be dancing. I shut my eyes not to see my image in obscene pupils: I would have liked to destroy my hearing not to hear the base comments about my good looks. I would have liked to stop up my nose not to smell the stench of souls; it was so strong that, next to it, the odor of corpses was perfume. I would have liked to lose all sense of taste not to feel in my mouth the repugnant one of my docility. But my two hands were tied and I could not kill myself. An arm slipped around my shoulder to hold me up, not to stroke me; the bindings around my legs fell: drunk with thirst and sun, I followed the stranger out of the death pit where those that even shame rejected would perish. I entered a house whose walls of beaten earth gave off a little muddy coolness; a pile of straw was given me as a bed. The man who had bought me held up my head to make me drink the last swallow of water that was left in the gourd. At first I thought it was love, but his hands went over my body only to dress my wounds. Then, since he was crying while rubbing me with a balm, I thought it was goodness. But I was wrong, Cebes: my savior was a slave trader: he was crying because my scars would make it impossible for me to fetch top prices in the bordellos of Athens; he was depriving himself of loving me for fear of becoming too attached to a fragile object, one you must get rid of right away while it is still perfect. Virtues, Cebes, don't all have the same motives and are not always pretty. This man took me to Corinth to be part of his cargo of slaves; he rented a horse to spare my feet. He couldn't prevent a number of his animals from drowning while

they were fording a river during a storm: we had
to proceed by foot on the blazing road that follows
the Isthmus of Corinth; each one of us, bent over
low enough to touch his shadow, carried the sun
like a heavy load. As we were coming out of a pine
forest, the horizon opened to reveal Athens: like a
chaste woman lying down, the city stretched between us and the sea. The temple on the hill slept
like a pink god. My misfortune had not made me
weep, but my tears flowed now for beauty. That
very evening, we went through the Dipylon Gate:
the streets smelled of urine, rancid oil, and dust
tumbled by the wind. Lace sellers were yelling at
crossroads, offering people the chance to strangle
themselves; no one took them up on it. House walls
hid the Parthenon from me. A lantern was burning
on the threshold of the whorehouse: all its rooms
were crammed with rugs and silver mirrors. The
luxury of my prison made me fear that I would be
kept in it forever. In order to dance, I had to slip
into a little round room furnished with low tables; I
was more nervous than on that morning of the
Olympic competition. As a child, I had danced in
meadows full of daffodils, choosing the freshest
flowers to step on. I danced on spit, on orange

peel, on glass splinters that drunks dropped. My painted nails shone within the orb of lamps; the vapor coming from hot food and human breath prevented me from seeing the clients' faces clearly enough to start hating them. I was a naked specter dancing for ghosts. Each time my heel hit the dirty floor, I drove my past, my future as a prince, further into the ground: my desperate dancing trampled Phaedo under my feet. One evening, a blond-lipped man came to sit at a table placed in full light; it didn't take the compliments of the proprietor for me to see that he was a member of the human Olympus. He was handsome like me, but to this multiple being, beauty was only one attribute; he lacked only immortality to be a god. All night long, this slightly drunk young man watched me dance. He came back the next day, but he was not alone. He was accompanied by a small, potbellied old man who looked like one of those toys ballasted by lead so that they stay upright in spite of children's attempts to topple them. One felt that this fat wily man had his center of gravity, his axis, his own density that would not be modified by the efforts of his detractors; the Absolute, which he had reached by a prodigal leap of his satyrlike legs, served him as pedestal. He was concrete as a tree trunk, ideal as a caricature, self-contained to the point of having become his own creator. Reason for this sophist was only a pure space in which he never tired of spinning ideas: Alcibiades was god, but this street vagabond seemed to be Universe. One looked for the hoofs of the celestial faun under his worn coat. This man swollen with wisdom rolled big pale eyes that looked like lenses that enlarge spiritual sins and virtues. The fixity of his gaze seemed to strengthen the muscles of my legs, the bones of my ankles, as though I had the wings of his thoughts at my heels. Before this Pan carved by a rough sculptor, a Pan who played the melodies of eternal life on the flutes of reason, my dancing stopped being a pretext to become a function, like the movement of the stars; and, as in the eyes of the debauched, wisdom is the supreme folly, spectators full of wine saw in my lightness the epitome of excess. Alcibiades clapped to summon the owner of the dance hall. My boss came forward, his hand cupped to receive gold. This man, who was in his element in vile dealings, not only counted on a profit of a few drachmas, but each vice sniffed out from the depth of human clay furnished him both the hope of a good bargain and the reassuring feeling of a base fraternity. My master called me over to let the clients appreciate the merchandise in the flesh; I sat down at their table, and next to this young man who looked like my lost pride, I instinctively recovered the gestures of my free childhood. Seeing that he no longer had any gold pieces tucked in his belt, Alcibiades unfastened two of his heavy bracelets to buy me. He was sailing the next day for the war in Sicily: already I dreamed of placing my chest like a sweet shield between him and danger. But this casual young god had acquired me only to please Socrates: for the first time in my life I felt rejected, and this humiliating refusal turned me over to Wisdom. The three of us went out into a street pitted by the last storm: Alcibiades disappeared into a thundering carriage. Socrates took his lantern and this meager star was more helpful than heaven's cold eyes. I followed my new master to his small house, where a slovenly woman awaited him, her mouth swollen with insults; unkempt children were squealing in the kitchen; the beds were full of vermin. Poverty, old age, his own ugliness, and the beauty of others flogged this Just Man with their viper straps: he was, like the rest of us, only a slave condemned to die. He felt oppressed by the ignominy of family affection—so often only an absence of respect. But rather than break free by sheer renunciations, motionless like a corpse afraid to hit his head on the ceiling of his tomb, he had understood that fate is only a hollow mold in which we pour our soul, and that life and death accept us as sculptors. This idle man imitated in turn his father the stonecutter and his mother the midwife: obstetrician, he brought souls into the world; statue maker, covered with objections as with a fine marble dust, he extricated a divine effigy from tender human blocks. His wisdom, multiple like the aspects of things, made up for him for the joys of debauchery, for athletic triumphs, for the exciting dangers adventurers seek on hazardous seas. Poor, he enjoyed the riches he would have possessed had he not devoted himself to invisible gains: chaste, he savored each night the taste of debaucheries he would have given himself to had he deemed them profitable to Socrates; ugly, he used, in a pure way, the beauty chance had bestowed on Charmides so that the quasi-grotesque body fate had lodged his soul in was only one of the many forms, no more precious than others, of the infinite Socrates. Like the freedom of the god allegedly creating worlds, his freedom lay in his disciples. He had understood that the whirlwind carrying my naked feet was allied to the immobility of his secret ecstasies: I saw him standing, indifferent to the stars, whose spinning did not increase his dizziness, a dark form gathered on the clear Attic night, easily bearing the atrocious icy wind blowing from the depths of God. Mornings, along lavender fields, I have followed this sublime procurer, who each day presented the youth of Athens with new naked truths. I escorted him along the Royal Portico, where death hooted for him like an owl under the guise of Anytus. The hemlock had grown in a nook of arid countryside: a potter from the agora fashioned the cup in which the poison would be poured. Slanders had ripened under the sun of Hate. I was the only one who knew the weariness of the wise man: only I had seen him rise from his wretched bed, pant as he leaned over to look for his sandals. But simple fatigue would not have made this seventy-year-old man give up the remaining portion of his breath. This man, who his whole life had swapped a clear truth for one more dazzling yet, a beautiful loved face for one more beautiful still, in the end found he could swap the slow and banal death that his arteries had in store for him against a more useful death, a fairer one, one engendered by his actions, one born of him like a devoted daughter who would come to tuck him into bed when night fell. This death, solid enough to last a few centuries around his memory, was inserted into the sequence of benevolent acts that made up his life and prolonged his way to an eternal life. It was fitting that on the hard foundation of laws, Athens should erect prouder and prouder temples to divinities ever more perfect, and it was fitting that he, the scorner sitting on porticos less beautiful than pure thought, should teach young men to trust only their souls. It was fitting that a servant dressed in mourning should come, by order of the Heliaea Jury, to give him the cup full of a bitter liquor; and it was also fitting that this peaceful death, a stain on so much azure, should make that azure appear purer yet. It may be that death had more charms for him than Alcibiades, since he did not stop it from slipping into his bed. It happened one evening at the time of the year when young beggars have their hands full of roses, at the hour the sun seems to cover Athens with kisses before saying farewell. A barque came into port folding its two wings, which were white like the swan of the god pilgrims pray to. The prison had been dug into the side of a rock; its open door brought the breeze and the cry of water carriers. From the bottom of the cavelike jail, the pale Parthenon shone for us like a divine Idea. Rich Crito was sulking, insulted that the Master had not allowed him to pave a way out with gold: Apollodorus was crying like a sniffling child: with a heavy heart, I held back my sighs: Plato was absent. Tablet in hand, Simmias was jotting down the last sayings of the doomed man. But already words seem to be leaving this calmed mouth only halfheartedly: perhaps the wise man understood that the alleys of Discourse he had wandered through his whole life led only to the edge of silence where the heartbeats of gods are heard. There always comes a moment when one learns to be quiet, perhaps because he has earned, at last, the right to listen; a moment when one stops doing things because one has learned to look fixedly at an unmoving thing, and this wisdom must be the wisdom of the dead. I was kneeling near the bed: my master put his hand on my long hair. I knew that his existence, devoted to sublime failure, drew its

principal virtues from amorous delights reached
only to be surpassed. Since, after all, flesh is the most
beautiful garment the soul can be dressed in, where
would Socrates be without Alcibiades' smile and
Phaedo's hair? To this old man who knew of the
world only the crossroads of Athens, a few loved
bodies had revealed not only the Absolute but also
the Universe. His slightly trembling hands were
wandering on the nape of my neck as though in a
valley alive with spring: guessing that eternity is
only a series of instants, each one unique, he felt
the silky blond form of eternal life flee under his
fingers. The jailer entered carrying the fatal cup
filled with the sap of the innocent plant: my master
emptied it: his shackles were removed; I slowly
massaged his congested, tired legs, and the last
thing he said was that voluptuousness is identical
to its sister, pain. I wept at these words that justified
my existence. When he lay down, I helped him to
cover his face with the folds of his old coat. For the
last time, I felt his nearsighted, kind glance on my
head, his sad-eyed-dog look. It was then, Cebes,
that he told us to sacrifice a rooster to the god of
Medicine: he left, taking with him the secret of
this supreme mischievousness. I understood that

this man, weary of a half century of wisdom, wanted to have a good nap before running the risk of Resurrection; uncertain of the future, happy once and for all to have been Socrates, he wanted to wring the neck of the messenger of recurring morning. The sun set: the cold reached his heart: to grow cold is the Sage's true death. As for us, the disciples ready to disperse, never to meet again, what we felt for each other was indifference, boredom, perhaps rancor: we were only scattered parts of the extinguished Philosopher. The seed of death contained in our life now quickly grew: pierced by Time's arrows, Alcibiades succumbed on the threshold of his maturity: Simmias rotted alive on the bench of a tavern, and wealthy Crito died of a stroke. Only I, having become invisible by sheer speed, keep on forming my endless parabola around a few tombs. Dancing on wisdom is dancing on sand. Each day, the sea of movement carries a bit of this arid ground to a spot where there is no life. For me, the immobility of death can only be a last stage of supreme speed: the pressure of the void will burst my heart. Already my dance goes beyond city ramparts, Acropolis terraces, and my body, turning like the spindle of the Fates, reels off its own death. My

---

foam-covered feet still land on the ever-undone crest of waves, but my forehead touches the stars, and the winds tear from me the rare memories that keep me from being naked. Socrates and Alcibiades are nothing more now than names, numbers, useless figures drawn on nothingness by the brushing of my feet. Ambition is only a lure; wisdom was wrong, even vice lied. There is neither virtue, nor pity, nor love, nor chastity, nor their forceful opposites; there is nothing but an empty shell dancing at the top of a joy which is also Grief, a flash of beauty in a shower of forms. Phaedo's long hair shines on the universal night like a sad meteor.

Love is a penalty. We are punished for not having been able to stay alone.

You must love someone to run the risk of suffering. I must love you very much to suffer you.

I can't help but see in my love a refined form of debauchery, a trick to pass time, to do without Time. Pleasure executes a forced landing in midair, the sound of its engines frenzied by the heart's last somersaults. Prayer rises in gliding flights; the soul leads the body in love's assumption. For assumption to be possible, there must be a god. You have just enough beauty, blindness, and exactingness to incarnate an all-powerful. Faute de mieux, I have made you the keystone of my universe.

*From a distance, your hair, your hands, your smile
evoke someone I adore. Who? Yourself.*

*Two o'clock in the morning. Rats, in the garbage
cans, gnaw at the dead day's remains: the city
belongs to ghosts, to murderers, to sleepwalkers.
Where are you, in what bed, in what dream? If I
ran into you, you would walk by without seeing
me, because we are not seen by our dreams. I am
not hungry: tonight I am unable to digest my life.
I am tired: I have walked all night to shake off
your memory. I am not sleepy: I am not even
hungry for death. Sitting on a bench, stupefied in
spite of myself by the approaching morning, I stop
reminding myself that I am trying to forget you. I
close my eyes. Thieves are only after our rings,
lovers our bodies, preachers our souls, murderers
our lives. They can take mine: I challenge them to
change a single thing in it. I throw my head back
to feel the movement of the leaves above me . . . I
am in a wood, in a field . . . Now Time is disguised
as a street sweeper, and God maybe as a ragpicker.
He the stingy one, he the stubborn one, he won't
allow one single pearl to be lost in the piles of
oystershells stacked before tavern doors. Our Father*

who art in Heaven . . . Will I ever see an old man in a brown overcoat come sit next to me; there will be mud on his feet because he crossed God knows what river to join me? He would flop on the bench, holding in his fist a very precious gift that would change everything. He would open his hand very slowly, one finger after the other, very carefully because it could fly off. What would he be holding? A bird, a seed, a knife, a key to open the can of the heart?

Wit? In grief? Why not, there is salt in tears.

Afraid of nothing? I am afraid of you.

CLYTEMNESTRA

OR CRIME

———

I will explain, gentlemen of the jury . . . I stand before countless eyes, circles of hands folded on knees, bare feet placed on stone, fixed pupils staring straight ahead, tightly closed mouths set in judgment. I stand before a statue-like assembly. I killed this man with an ax, in a bathtub, with the help of my wretched lover, who couldn't even grab hold of his feet. You know my story; there isn't one among you who didn't repeat it twenty times at the end of long meals while your servants yawned, and there isn't one among your wives who didn't at least one night of her life dream of being Clytemnestra. Your criminal thoughts, your secret envies come down, row after row, toward me, so that a horrible back-and-forth motion makes you my conscience and me your scream. You came here so that the playing out of the murder could be repeated before your eyes a little faster than in reality, because, due back home for the evening meal, all you can spare is a few hours to hear me weep. And in this short space my actions and their motives must be blown up in full view even though it took me forty years to assert them. I waited for this man before he even had a name, a face, when he was still only my distant misfortune. I searched among the crowd of the living for the creator of my future delights: I looked at men only as one stares at people passing by in a train station, to be sure they are not what you are waiting for. He's the one my wet-nurse swaddled me for when I came out of my mother. It's to keep the accounts of his prosperous household that I learned math at school. It's to welcome the stranger who would make me his servant that I wove these bridal sheets and gold streamers; I applied myself so hard that a few drops of my blood fell here and there on the velvety material. My parents chose him for me, but even if kidnapped by him without their knowledge, I would still have obeyed the wishes of my mother and father, since our tastes come from them, and the man we love is always the one our great-grandmothers dreamed of. I let the future of our children be sacrificed to his own personal ambitions: I didn't

even cry when my daughter died of them. I agreed
to melt into his destiny like a fruit in his mouth, so
as to bring him nothing but sweetness. Gentlemen
of the jury, when you knew him he was already
thickset by fame, aged by a decade of war, a sort of
enormous idol worn down by the caresses of Asiatic
women, splattered by the mud of trenches. I'm the
only one who knew him during his godlike years.
It was sweet to me to bring him on a big copper
tray the glass of water that would refresh him; it
was sweet to me to prepare in the hot kitchen the
dishes that would gratify his hunger and fill him
with blood. Heavy with the weight of human sowing, it was sweet to me to put my hands on my big
belly, in which my children were rising like dough.
At night, when he returned from hunting, I threw
myself on his golden chest with joy. But men are
not made to spend their entire lives warming themselves at the same domestic fires. He went away
toward new conquests and left me standing like
a big deserted house filled with the ticking of a
useless clock. Time spent far from him was idle
time, flowing drop by drop, or by spurts like lost
blood, leaving me each month more bereft of the
future. Drunken soldiers on leave told me of his life

in officers' quarters: the army of the Orient was in-
fested with women: Jewesses from Salonika, Ar-
menians from Tiflis whose blue eyes under dark
lids evoked water streaming deep in dark caves,
Turkish women heavy and sweet like those pastries
made with honey. I received letters on birthdays;
my life was spent watching the road for the limping
footsteps of the mailman. During the day I fought
against anguish, at night against desire, but always
against the emptiness, this cowardly side of unhappiness. The years went by like a procession of
widows along deserted streets: the village square
was dark with women in mourning. I envied these
women having only the earth as rival and knowing
at least that their men slept alone. In his stead, I
watched over the fieldwork and had the coast pa-
trolled; I garnered the harvest; I had the heads of
highwaymen nailed to the stake in the market; I
used my rifle to shoot crows; with my brown linen
gaiters I beat the flanks of my hunting mare. Little
by little, I took the place of the man I missed and
who haunted me. I ended up looking with his eyes
at the white neck of servant girls. Aegisthus raced
beside me in fallow fields; his adolescence coin-
cided with my widowhood; he was almost old

enough to join the men; he reminded me of summer vacations long ago when cousins shared kisses in the woods. I considered him less a lover than my child fathered by absence. I paid for his saddles and his horses. I was unfaithful to my husband by imitating him. Aegisthus was to me the equivalent of these Asiatic women or the ignominious Argynnes. Gentlemen of the jury, there is only one man in the world: the rest, for each woman, are only mistakes or sad last resorts. And adultery is often only a desperate form of fidelity. If I cheated on someone, it's certainly poor Aegisthus. I needed him to know just how irreplaceable the one I loved was. Tired of caressing him, I would climb the tower to share the watchman's insomnia. On one such night, three hours before dawn, the eastern horizon caught fire. Troy was burning: the wind coming from Asia carried sparks and clouds of ashes across the sea; sentinels lighted fires in celebration on the summits; the mountains of Athos, Olympus, Pindus, and Erymanthos were blazing like pyres; at last a flame was lighted on the little hill that for twenty-five years had blocked my horizon. I saw the helmeted head of the watchman bend to concentrate on messages whispered by the waves: somewhere on the sea, a man bedecked with gold was leaning his elbows against the prow, letting each circling of the propeller bring him closer to his wife and absent home. Going down the tower, I grabbed a knife. I wanted to kill Aegisthus, have the bedstead and the pavement of the room washed, bring out from the bottom of a trunk the dress I was wearing when he left, eliminate, at last, these ten years like a simple zero in the sum total of my days. Walking in front of the mirror, I stopped to smile: suddenly I saw myself, and the sight reminded me that I had gray hair. Gentlemen of the jury, ten years is nothing to sneer at; it's longer than the distance between the city of Troy and the castle of Mycenae; it's higher than the place where we are, since we can only go down and not up in Time. It's like in nightmares: each step we take removes us further from our goal, instead of bringing us closer. Instead of his young wife, the king would find a fat cook on the threshold; he would congratulate her on the good condition of the chicken coops and the cellars: all I could expect was a few cold kisses. If I had the heart for it, I would have killed myself before the hour of his return, to avoid reading on his face his disappointment in finding me so faded. But I wanted at least to see him again before dying. Aegisthus was crying in my bed, frightened like a guilty child who feels the father's punishments coming; I drew near him; in my most sweetly lying voice I told him nothing would be known of our nights together and that his uncle had no reason to stop loving him. I was hoping, on the contrary, that he already knew everything and that wrath and the taste for revenge would thus grant me room in his thoughts. To be even surer, I added to the mail that would reach him on board an anonymous letter exaggerating my sins. I sharpened the knife that was to open my heart. I was hoping that to strangle me he would use his two hands so often kissed: at least I would be dying in a sort of embrace. The day came when the boat was finally moored in the port of Nauplia amid a great uproar of fanfares and hurrahs; the slopes covered with red poppies seemed decked out by order of the summer; the children of the village had been given a holiday by their teacher; church bells were ringing. I was waiting before the threshold of the Lioness Gate; a pink parasol masked my pallor. The wheels of the carriage squeaked on the steep slope;

the villagers harnessed themselves to the carriage shafts to relieve the horses. At a turn in the road, at last, I saw the top of the carriage clear the quickset hedge and I noticed that my man was not alone. Next to him he had a sort of Turkish sorceress he had chosen as his part of the loot, even though, having been toyed with by soldiers, she looked a little the worse for wear. She was still somewhat of a child; she had beautiful deep blue eyes, her bruises looked like tattoos; he was stroking her arm to keep her from crying. He helped her out of the car; he kissed me coldly, telling me that he relied on my generosity not to mistreat this young woman whose father and mother were dead; he shook hands with Aegisthus. My husband, too, had changed. He panted when he walked; his big red neck spilled over the collar of his shirt; his beard, painted red, was lost in the folds of his chest. Yet he was handsome, but as a bull is handsome, rather than as a god. He climbed the steps of the entrance hall with us; these I had covered with a scarlet runner as I did on my wedding day, so that my spilled blood would not show. He hardly looked at me; at dinner, he did not notice that I had had all his favorite dishes prepared; he drank two, three glasses of liquor; the torn envelope of the anonymous letter was sticking out of one of his pockets; he kept on winking at Aegisthus. During dessert, he muddled drunken jokes about women who let themselves be comforted. The evening seemed interminably long on the mosquito-infested terrace; he was speaking Turkish with his mistress; it appeared that she was the daughter of a tribal chief; a move she made showed me that she was pregnant. Perhaps it was by him or by one of the soldiers who had laughingly dragged her from her own camp and with a whip driven her to our side of the trenches. It appeared that she had the gift of telling the future: to amuse us, she read our palms. Thereupon she paled and her teeth chattered. I also, gentlemen of the jury, knew the future. All women know it; they always expect things to end badly. He was in the habit of taking a warm bath before going to sleep. I went up to get everything ready: the sound of the water running allowed me to weep out loud. The bath was heated by wood. An ax used to split logs was lying on the floor; I don't know why I hid it behind the towel racks. For a moment I felt like disguising everything as an accident that would leave no clues, so that the petroleum lamp would be the only witness. But I wanted to force him, as he died, to at least look me in the face; I killed him only for that, to force him to realize that I was not a thing of no importance that you could drop or hand over to the first comer. I called Aegisthus softly: he became livid as soon as I opened my mouth: I ordered him to wait for me on the landing. The other one climbed the stairs heavily; he took off his shirt; his skin, in the warm water, became purple all over. I was rubbing soap on his neck: I was shaking so hard that the soap kept slipping out of my hands; he was short of breath and ordered me roughly to open the window that was too high for me to reach; I yelled at Aegisthus to come help me. As soon as he was in the room, I locked the door. The other one did not see me, for his back was turned to us. Clumsily I struck the first blow that only nicked his shoulder; he stood straight up; his bloated face became blotched with dark spots; he was bellowing like an ox; terrified, Aegisthus seized his knees as if to beg his pardon. My husband lost his balance on the slippery bottom of the bathtub and fell like a log, face in the water, with a gurgling noise that sounded like a rattle. That's when I gave him the second blow; the one that split his forehead open. But I do believe that he was already dead: he was only a limp and warm rag. There has been talk of red floods: in truth, he bled very little. I shed more blood giving birth to his son. After his death, we killed his mistress: it was the more generous thing to do if she was in love with him. The villagers took our side; they kept quiet. My son was too young to give free rein to his hatred of Aegisthus. A few weeks went by: I should have felt at peace, but you know, gentlemen of the jury, that there is no end to it, that everything always starts all over again. I started waiting for him again: he came back. Don't shake your heads, I'm telling you that he came back. He who for ten years didn't bother taking a week off to come back from Troy came back from death. In vain did I cut off his feet to stop him from leaving the cemetery; that did not prevent him from sneaking into my room at night carrying his feet under his arms like house-breakers carrying their shoes in order not to make any noise. His shadow covered me; he didn't even seem to notice Aegisthus' presence. Later my son denounced me to the police; but my son is still his ghost, his fleshy specter. I thought that at least in jail I would have peace, but he still comes back:

you would think that he prefers my dark cell to his tomb. I know that in the end my head will roll on the village square and that Aegisthus' head will also fall under the same blade. It's funny, gentlemen of the jury, one would even say that you have already judged me. But I have learned by experience that the dead do not lie still: I will rise again, dragging Aegisthus on my heels like a sad greyhound. I will go along the roads at night seeking God's justice. I will find this man in a corner of my hell; once again I'll scream with joy under his first kisses. Then he'll leave me: he'll go conquering a province of Death. Since Time is the blood of the living, Eternity must be shadow blood. My own eternity will be wasted waiting for his return, so that I will soon be the most livid of ghosts. Then he will come back to deride me; he will caress his yellow Turkish witch used to playing with the bones of the dead. What can you do? You can't kill a dead man.

Not to be loved anymore is to become invisible; now you don't notice that I have a body.

Between us and death there is sometimes only the width of one single person. Remove this person and there would be only death.

How dull it would have been to be happy!

I owe each of my tastes to the influence of chance friendships, as though I could only accept the world from human hands. From Hyacinth I have this liking of flowers, from Philip of travel, from Celeste of medicine, from Alexis of laces. From you, why not a predilection for death?

SAPPHO

OR SUICIDE

I have just seen, reflected in the mirrors of a theater box, a woman called Sappho. She is pale as snow, as death, or as the clear face of a woman who has leprosy. And since she wears rouge to hide this whiteness, she looks like the corpse of a murdered woman with a little of her own blood on her cheeks. To shun daylight, her eyes recede from the arid lids, which no longer shade them. Her long curls come out in tufts like forest leaves falling under precocious storms; each day she tears out new gray hairs, and soon there will be enough of these white silken threads to weave her shroud. She weeps for her youth as if for a woman who betrayed her, for her childhood as if for a little girl she has lost. She is skinny; when she steps into her bath, she turns away from the mirror, from the sight of her sad breasts. She wanders from city to city with three big trunks full of false pearls and bird wreckage. She is an acrobat, just as in ancient times she was a poetess, because the particular shape of her lungs forces her to choose a trade that is practiced in midair. In the circus at night, under the devouring eyes of a mindless public, and in a space encumbered with pulleys and masts, she fulfills her contract; she is a star. Outside, upstaged by the luminous letters of posters stuck to the wall, her body is part of that ghostly circle currently in vogue that soars above the gray cities. She's a magnetic creature, too winged for the ground, too corporal for the sky, whose wax-rubbed feet have broken the pact that binds us to the earth: Death waves her dizzy scarves but does not fluster her. Naked, spangled with stars, from afar she looks like an athlete who won't admit being an angel lest his perilous leaps be underrated; from close up, draped in long robes that give her back her wings, she looks like a female impersonator. She alone knows that her chest holds a heart too heavy and too big to be lodged elsewhere than in a broad bosom: this weight, hidden at the bottom of a bone cage, gives each of her springs into the void the mortal taste of danger. Half eaten by this implacable tiger, she secretly tries to be the tamer of her heart. She was

born on an island and that is already a beginning
of solitude; then her profession intervened, forcing
on her a sort of lofty isolation every night; fated to
be a star, she lies on her stage board, half un-
dressed, exposed to the winds of the abyss, and
suffers from the lack of tenderness as from the lack
of pillows. Men in her life have only been steps
of a ladder she had to climb, often dirtying her feet.
The director, the trombone player, the publicity
agent, all made her sick of waxed mustaches, cigars,
liqueurs, striped ties, leather wallets—the exterior
attributes of virility that make women dream.
Only young women's bodies would still be soft
enough, supple enough, fluid enough to let themselves be handled by this strong angel who would
playfully pretend to drop them in midair. She can't
hold them very long in this abstract space bordered
on all sides by trapeze bars: quickly frightened by
this geometry changing into wingbeats, all of them
soon give up acting as her sky companion. She has
to come down to earth, to their level, to share their
ragged, patchy lives, so that affection ends up like
a Saturday pass, a twenty-four-hour leave a sailor
spends with easy women. Suffocating in these
rooms no bigger than alcoves, she opens the door to

the void with the hopeless gesture of a man forced, by love, to live among dolls. All women love one woman: they love themselves madly, consenting to find beauty only in the form of their own body. Sappho's eyes, farsighted in sorrow, looked further away. She expects of young women what self-adorning idolatrous coquettes expect of mirrors: a smile answering her trembling smile, until the breath from lips moving closer and closer obscures the reflection and clouds the crystal. Narcissus loves what he is. Sappho bitterly worships in her companions what she has not been. Poor, held in contempt, which is the other side of celebrity, and having only the perspectives of the abyss in stock, she caresses happiness on the bodies of her less threatened friends. The veils of communicants carrying their souls outside themselves make her dream of a brighter childhood than hers had been; when one has run out of illusions, one can still lend others a sinless childhood. The pallor of these girls awakens in her the almost unbelievable memory of virginity. In Gyrinno, she loved pride, and lowered herself to kiss the girl's feet. Anactoria's love brought her the taste of French fries eaten by handfuls in amusement parks, of rides on the wooden horses of carousels, and brought her the sweet feel of straw, tickling the neck of the beautiful girl lying down in haystacks. In Attys, she loved misfortune. She met Attys in the center of a big city, asphyxiated by the breath of its crowds and by the fog of its river; her mouth still smelled of the ginger candy she had been chewing. Soot stains stuck to her cheeks shiny with tears: she was running on a bridge, wearing a coat of fake otter; her shoes had holes; her face like that of a young goat had a haggard sweetness. To explain why her lips were pinched and pale like the scar of an old wound, why her eyes looked like sick turquoises, Attys had three different stories that were after all only three aspects of the same misfortune: her boyfriend, whom she saw every Sunday, had left her because one evening she wouldn't let him caress her in a taxi; a girlfriend who let her sleep on the couch of her student room had turned her out, accusing her wrongly of trying to steal her fiancé's heart; and finally, her father beat her. Attys was afraid of everything: of ghosts, of men, of the number 13, of the green eyes of cats. The hotel dining room dazzled her like a temple where she felt obliged to speak only in a whisper; the bathroom

made her clap her hands in amazement. Sappho
spends the money she has saved for years through
suppleness and temerity for this whimsical girl. She
makes circus directors hire this mediocre artist who
can only juggle flower bouquets. With the regu-
larity of change that is the essence of life for nomadic artists and sad profligates, together they tour
the arenas and stages of all capitals. Each morning,
in the furnished rooms rented so that Attys will
avoid the promiscuity of hotels full of too rich
clients, they mend their costumes and the runs in
their tight silk stockings. Sappho has nursed this
sick child so often, has so many times warded off
men who would tempt her, that her gloomy love
imperceptibly takes on a maternal cast, as though
fifteen years of sterile voluptuousness had produced
this child. The young men in tuxedos met in the
halls of theater boxes, all recall to Attys the friend
whose repulsed kisses she perhaps misses: Sappho
has heard her talk so often of Philip's beautiful silk
shirts, of his blue cuff links, of the shelves of porno-
graphic albums decorating his room in Chelsea,
that she now has as clear a picture of this fastidi-
ously dressed businessman as of the few lovers she
couldn't avoid slipping into her life. She stows

him away absentmindedly among her worst memories. Little by little, Attys' eyelids take on a lavender hue; she gets letters at a post-office box and she tears them up after reading them; she seems strangely well informed about the business trips that might make the young man run into them, by chance, on their nomadic road. It is painful to Sappho not to be able to give Attys anything more than a back room in life, and to know that only fear keeps the little fragile head leaning on her strong shoulder. Sappho, embittered by all the tears she had the courage never to shed, realizes that all she can offer her friends is a tender form of despair; her only excuse is to tell herself that love, in all its forms, has nothing better to offer shy creatures, and were Attys to leave, she would not find more happiness somewhere else. One night Sappho, arms full of flowers picked for Attys, comes home later than usual. The concierge looks at her differently than she ordinarily does as she walks by; suddenly the spirals of the staircase look like serpent rings. Sappho notices that the milk carton is not in its usual place on the doormat; as soon as she is in the entrance hall, she smells the odor of cologne and blond tobacco. She notices in the kitchen the ab-

sence of an Attys busy frying tomatoes; in the bathroom the want of a young woman naked and playing
with bathwater; in the bedroom the removal of an
Attys ready to let herself be rocked. Facing the
mirrors of the wide-open wardrobe, she weeps over
the disappearance of the beloved girl's underwear.
A blue cuff link lying on the floor reveals the cause
of this departure, which Sappho stubbornly refuses
to accept as final, afraid that it could kill her.
Once again, she is trampling alone on city arenas,
avidly scanning the theater boxes for a face her
folly prefers to all bodies. After a few years, during
one of her tours in the East, she learns that Philip
is now director of a company that sells Oriental
tobaccos; he has just been married to a rich and
imposing woman who couldn't be Attys. Rumor
has it that the girl has joined a dance company.
Once again, Sappho makes the rounds of Middle
East hotels; each doorman has his own way of
being insolent, impudent, or servile; she checks out
the pleasure spots where the smell of sweat poisons
perfumes, the bars where an hour of stupor in
alcohol and human heat leaves no more trace than
a wet circle left by a glass on a black wooden table.
She carries her search even as far as going to the

Salvation Army, in the vain hope of finding Attys impoverished and ready to let herself be loved. In Istanbul, she happens to sit, every night, next to a casually dressed young man who passes himself off as an employee of a travel agency; his slightly dirty hand lazily holds up the weight of his forehead. They exchange those banal words that are often used between strangers as a bridge to love. He says his name is Phaon, claims he is the son of a Greek woman from Smyrna and of a sailor in the British fleet: once again, Sappho's heart quickens when she hears the delightful accent so often kissed on Attys' lips. Behind him stand memories of escape, of poverty, and of dangers unrelated to wars and more secretly connected to the laws of his own heart. He, too, seems to belong to a threatened race; one that is allowed to exist through a precarious and ever provisional permissiveness. Not having a residence visa, this young man has his own difficulties; he's a smuggler dealing in morphine, perhaps an agent of the secret police; he lives in a world of secret meetings and passwords, a world Sappho cannot penetrate. He doesn't need to tell her his story to establish a fraternity of misfortune between them. She tells him her sorrows; she goes on and on about Attys. He thinks he has met her; he vaguely remembers seeing a naked girl juggling flowers in a cabaret of Pera. He owns a little sailboat that he uses on Sundays for outings on the Bosphorus; together they go looking in all sad cafés along the shore, in restaurants of the island, in the modest boarding-houses on the Asian coast that poor foreigners live in. Seated at the stern, Sappho watches this hand-some male face, which is now her only human sun, waver in the light of a lantern. She finds in his features certain traits once loved in the runaway girl: the same pouting mouth that a mysterious bee seems to have stung; the same little hard forehead under different hair that this time seemed to have been dipped in honey, the same eyes looking like greenish turquoises but framed by a tanned, rather than livid, face, so that the pale brown-haired girl seems to have been simply the wax lost in casting this bronze and golden god. Surprised, Sappho finds herself slowly preferring these shoulders rigid as trapeze bars, these hands hardened by the contact of oars, this entire body holding just enough fem-inine softness for her to love it. Lying down on the bottom of the boat, she yields to the new sensations of the floodwaters parted by this ferryman. Now

124

she only mentions Attys to tell him that the lost girl looked like him but wasn't as handsome: Phaon accepts these compliments with a mocking but worried satisfaction. She tears up, in front of him, a letter in which Attys announces that she is coming back; she doesn't even bother to make out the return address. He watches her doing this with a faint smile on his trembling lips. For the first time, she neglects the discipline of her demanding profession, she interrupts the exercises which put every muscle under the control of the spirit; they dine together; and surprisingly, she eats a little too much. She only has a few days left with him in this city; her commitments have her soaring in other skies. Finally he consents to spend the last evening with her in the little apartment she rents near the port. She watches him come and go in the cluttered room, he is like a voice mingling clear and deep notes. Unsure of his moves, as though afraid of breaking fragile illusions, Phaon leans over the portraits of Attys for a better look. Sappho sits down on the Viennese sofa covered with Turkish embroideries; she presses her face in her hands like someone trying to erase memories. This woman who until now took upon herself the choice, the

offer, the seduction, the protection of her more
vulnerable girlfriends, relaxes and, falling, yields
limply, at last, to the weight of her own sex and of
her own heart. She is happy that, from now on, all
she has to do with a lover is to make the gesture of
acceptance. She listens to the young man prowl in
the next room; there, the whiteness of a bed is
sprawled like a hope remaining, in spite of everything, miraculously open; she hears him uncork
flasks on the dresser, rummage in drawers with the
ease of a housebreaker or a boyfriend who feels he is
allowed everything. He opens the folding doors of
the wardrobe, where, among a few ruffles left by
Attys, Sappho's dresses hang like women who have
killed themselves. Suddenly the ghostly shudder of
a silken sound draws near like a dangerous caress.
She rises, turns around; the beloved creature has
wrapped himself in a robe Attys left behind: the
thin silk gauze worn on naked flesh accentuates the
quasi-feminine gracefulness of the dancer's long
legs; relieved of its confining men's clothing, this
flexible body is almost a woman's body. This Phaon,
comfortable in his impersonation, is nothing more
than a stand-in for the beautiful absent nymph;
once again, it's a girl coming toward her with a

crystal laugh. Distraught, Sappho runs to the door
to escape from this fleshly ghost who will only give
her the same sad kisses. Outside, she charges into the
swell of bodies and runs down the streets leading
to the sea; they are littered with debris and garbage.
She realizes that no encounter holds her salvation,
since, no matter where she goes, she runs into Attys
again. This overwhelming face blocks all openings
but those leading to death. Night falls like a weariness confusing her memory; a little blood endures
next to the sunset. Suddenly she hears cymbals
clashing as though fever hit them in her heart; a
long-standing habit has brought her back, un-
wares, to the circus at the very hour when she
struggles with the angel of dizziness each night.
For the last time, she is intoxicated by this wild-
beast odor that has been the odor of her life, by
this music like that of love, loud and discordant. A
wardrobe woman lets her into the dressing room,
which she enters now as if condemned to death; she
strips as if for God; she rubs white makeup all over
herself to become a ghost; she snaps the choker of
memory around her neck. An usher, dressed in
black, arrives to tell her that her hour has come; she
climbs the rope ladder of her celestial scaffold: she

is fleeing skywards from the mockery of believing that there had been a young man. She removes herself from the yells of orange vendors, from the cutting laughter of pink children, from the skirts of dancers, from the mesh of human nets. With one pull, she brings herself to the last support her will to die will allow: the trapeze bar swinging in mid-air transforms this creature, tired of being only half woman, into a bird; she glides, sea gull of her own abyss, hanging by one foot, under the gaze of a public which does not believe in tragedy. Her skill goes against her; no matter how she tries, she can't lose her balance; shady equestrian, Death has her vault the next trapeze. She climbs at last higher than the spotlights: spectators can no longer applaud her, since now they can't see her. Hanging on to the ropes that pull the canopy painted with stars, she can only continue to surpass herself by bursting through her sky. Under her, the ropes, the pulleys, the winches of her fate now mastered, squeak in the wind of dizziness; space leans and pitches as on a stormy sea; the star-filled firmament rocks between mast yards. From here, music is only a smooth swell washing over all memory. Her eyes no longer distinguish between red and green lights;

blue spotlights, sweeping over the dark crowd, bring out, here and there, naked feminine shoulders that look like tender rocks. Hanging on to her death as to an overhanging ledge, Sappho looks for a place to fall and chooses a spot beyond the netting where the mesh will not hold her. Her own acrobatic performance occupies only half of the immense vague arena; in the other half, where seals and clowns carry on, nothing has been set up to prevent her from dying. Sappho dives, arms spread as if to grasp half of infinity; she leaves behind her only the swinging of a rope as proof of having left the sky. But those failing at life run the risk of missing their suicide. Her oblique fall is broken by a lamp shining like a blue jellyfish. Stunned but safe, she is thrown by the impact toward the netting that pulls and repulses the foamy light; the meshes give but do not yield under the weight of this statue fished out from the bottom of the sky. And soon roustabouts will only have to haul onto the sand this marble pale body streaming with sweat like a drowning woman pulled from the sea.

I will not kill myself. The dead are so quickly forgotten.

One can only raise happiness on a foundation of despair. I think I will be able to start building.

Let no one be accused of my life.

It's not a question of suicide. It's only a question of beating a record.

Phoenix Fiction titles from Chicago

The Bridge on the Drina by Ivo Andrić
Concrete by Thomas Bernhard
Correction by Thomas Bernhard
Gargoyles by Thomas Bernhard
The Lime Works by Thomas Bernhard
Old Masters by Thomas Bernhard
Wittgenstein's Nephew by Thomas Bernhard
Woodcutters by Thomas Bernhard
Yes by Thomas Bernhard
The Last, Long Journey by Roger Cleeve
Acts of Theft by Arthur A. Cohen
A Hero in His Time by Arthur A. Cohen
In the Days of Simon Stern by Arthur A. Cohen
Solomon's Folly by Leslie Croxford
The Old Man and the Bureaucrats by Mircea Eliade
In the Time of Greenbloom by Gabriel Fielding
Through Streets Broad and Narrow by Gabriel Fielding
Convergence by Jack Fuller
Concluding by Henry Green
Pictures from an Institution by Randall Jarrell
The Survival of the Fittest by Pamela Hansford Johnson
A Bird in the House by Margaret Laurence
The Diviners by Margaret Laurence
The Fire-Dwellers by Margaret Laurence
A Jest of God by Margaret Laurence
The Stone Angel by Margaret Laurence
Fiela's Child by Dalene Matthee
The Conquerors by André Malraux
The Walnut Trees of Altenberg by André Malraux
The Bachelor of Arts by R. K. Narayan
The Dark Room by R. K. Narayan
The English Teacher by R. K. Narayan
Swami and Friends by R. K. Narayan
A Father's Words by Richard Stern
Golk by Richard Stern
An Innocent Millionaire by Stephen Vizinczey
In Praise of Older Women by Stephen Vizinczey
Lord Byron's Doctor by Paul West
The Painted Canoe by Anthony Winkler
A Coin in Nine Hands by Marguerite Yourcenar
Fires by Marguerite Yourcenar
Two Lives and a Dream by Marguerite Yourcenar